Filthy Professor

Filthy, Volume 3

Amy Brent

Published by Amy Brent, 2021.

FILTHY PROFESSOR

First edition. March 1, 2021.

ISBN: 979-8201111472

Written by Amy Brent.

Also by Amy Brent

Filthy

Filthy Boss

Filthy Doctor

Filthy Professor

Filthy Seal

Filthy Cowboy

Filthy Daddy

Filthy Coach

Forbidded

The Doctor's Fake Marriage

Forbidden

Fake Fiance

One More Chance

Crave Me

My Best Friend's Dad

The Doctor's Fake Marriage

Dad's Best Friend

Forbidden Fantasies

Daddy's Business Partner

Daddy's Friend

Daddy O

Climbing His Corporate Ladder

Taken By Daddy's Boss

Filthy Liar

Standalone

Teachers' Pet

Filthy Box Set

Knocked Up By My Brother's Best Friend

My Best Friend's Brother

My Best Friend's Ex

Say You're Mine

Club Desire Box Set

My Boyfriend's Dad

Fighting For Her

Forbidden Love Box Set

Love Undercover

Friends With Benefits

A Royal Menage

Baby Fever

Vegas Baby

Brother's Best Friend for Christmas

Christmas With My Best Friend's Dad

My Son's Sitter

Single Dad's Christmas Present

Surrendering To 3 Alphas

Because I Love You
Catching Up With Daddy
Claiming Cinderella
Double Trouble
First Love
First Time
Knocked Up By My Brother's Best Friend
My Best Friend's Boyfriend
Pretend Daddy
Redemption
Roomies With Benefits
Royally Yours
Rub Me The Right Way
Show Stopper
That One Night
The Baby Contract
Truth Or Dare
Santa's Naughty List
Quickie on Christmas
Con Man

Table of Contents

FILTHY PROFESSOR

by

Amy Brent

That's it, I can't stand it anymore! I've spent months trying to get Professor Logan Clark to notice me. I dress sexy, I gaze into his eyes, I lick my lips when he looks at me. I want to get him out of his classroom and out of his clothes for a little private, one-on-one tutoring...

COURTNEY SHAW: I'm a smoking hot red head with a sex drive that would make a porn star blush and a major daddy complex. Older men are my thing, and lots of them have sampled the sweet treats I have in my panties. So why isn't Logan Clark jumping at the chance to be with me? Even after our little oral exam in the restroom he keeps pushing me away. Is this his idea of torture? Well, two can play at that game...

LOGAN CLARK: Damn this girl, doesn't she understand that there are rules against professors having sex with students, no matter how smoking hot and sexy they are? She doesn't seem to care that screwing her could get me fired. I'm not going to risk my job just to have sex with her. No way. Not even after she drops a wet thong on my desk and shows up naked at my door. I've worked too hard to get where I am at this school. I'm not going blow it all for her. At least that's what I keep telling myself...

CHAPTER ONE: Courtney Shaw

I bit my lower lip as I watched him pace across the front of the classroom with his head down, deep in thought, talking with his hands, trying to explain an advanced accounting theory to the moron who always sat on the front row and always asked questions everyone else already knew the answers to.

Professor Logan Clark was tall, like six-foot-something, with sandy blond hair that curled over his collar and hung over his forehead like a teenager's. He jerked his head to the side sometimes to get it out of his eyes.

Speaking of eyes, his were like two piercing blue orbs that lasered into my soul when he glanced my way. Sometimes I would ask a question just to get him to look at me. Sadly, he would just answer the question and move on, seemingly without noticing that I had been licking my lips and soaking the crotch of my panties the entire time he was looking at me.

I studied his face, though I had already committed every inch of it to memory. He had a deep tan, as did most everyone here in southern California in the late summertime. I'd never seen him without the stubble of a five o'clock shadow on his cheeks and chin. I thought it was so fucking sexy, the way he scratched his chin when he was trying to make a point.

He always wore baggy jeans that hung low on his narrow hips and tan work boots that looked like they'd been taken off of a migrant worker back in the seventies (I'm only 22, so that seems like a thousand years ago).

I could tell that he was muscular beneath the wrinkled white shirt and crooked knit tie he always wore. He wore the sleeves rolled up to his elbows, exposing the sinewy muscles in his forearms and hands. And he always wore the shirt untucked, which frustrated me to no end because it kept me from checking out his package. Rumor was that he was hung like a horse. Well, you certainly couldn't tell it by looking at him in the classroom.

His round shoulders and a thick chest pushed against the thin material of the white shirt. The shirt was tight across his broad back, looking like it might split at the seams if he were to flex his muscles. I'd spent months wondering what he looked like beneath those baggy professor clothes. And I wasn't alone. All the girls talked about him after class. He was out favorite topic.

Wonder what would Professor Clark looks like naked?

Do you think he's really hairy or is would his chest be baby smooth?

Do you think his pubes are as blond as the hair on his head or are they be darker, like the stubble on his chin?

And do you think his pubes are thick and curly, or do you think he keeps them neatly trimmed?

Or, be still my heart, do you think he's shaved clean... down there?

How long do you think his cock is?

Do you think his cock is circumcised with a big mushroom head?

Or maybe his cock is as natural as the day he was born, more snakelike than bulbous fuck stick?

I barely listened to their school girl chatter because none of that stuff mattered to me. I'd take Logan Clark any way that I could get him. I'd sat in his accounting class for three months dreaming about having his cock in my mouth and in my cunt, regardless of its shape or size.

And now I was running out of time to make my fantasies come true.

There were only two weeks left in this semester and I would be graduating in a month and taking a job with a big accounting firm in Chicago, working for my stepdad, Earl Shaw. I'd already signed the offer letter and they expected me to start in the fall.

It was a done deal and my mom would kill me if I tried to back out on it now; even if staying in Cali to fuck Logan Clark was the reason.

Time to grow up, Courtney, she liked to say. And she was right. I was twenty-two. Time to put all that silly stuff behind me.

I'd move away from sunny southern California for good, without ever getting to know Logan Clark in the way that I wanted so desperately to know him.

I dreamt of him when I slept.

I fantasized about him when I made myself cum with the goodies in my secret toy box.

But other than answering my occasion question about accounting, he'd never even looked my way.

Maybe my roommate, Mindy, was right.

If I wanted to fuck Professor Logan Clark before I left Golden State for good, I'd better get my sweet ass in gear.

CHAPTER TWO: Courtney

Okay, I know what you must be thinking: wow, what a skanky slut this bitch must be, sitting in class thinking about sucking her professor's cock. Get your mind out of the gutter, you little whore, and on your studies where they belong!

The truth is, I'm not a skanky slut or a little whore, at least not in public. I'm just a normal, healthy, twenty-two-year-old woman with a daddy complex and a sex drive that would make a porn star jealous.

I couldn't help it. For as long as I could remember, even in my early teens, my desire for sex had been overwhelming.

I started letting boys feel my titties over my shirt and rub my crotch when I was thirteen. I let a boy slip his hand under my shirt to feel the round globes of my breasts when I was just fourteen.

My boobs came early, like a prize from Mother Nature, so why should I have deprived boys the chance to feel me up and deprived myself the joy of experimentation.

I remembered when one boy whose name I couldn't even remember squeezed my nipples so hard it made me whimper in pain. He quickly pulled his hand away and started apologizing. I put his hand back on my tit and told him to keep doing what he'd been doing because it felt fucking awesome.

The first boy to slip his hands inside my jeans and panties and feel the hot moisture of my young pussy, was Bobby Rigsby, who was fifteen at the time. He shot his load in his pants as I tugged on his short cock through his jeans. He was so embarrassed he ran away without another word, leaving me standing under the bleachers during the football game with the smell of his cum on my fingers and a fire burning between my legs. I licked him off my fingers and went to get a snow cone. I was barely fifteen.

I became a sexual explorer in high school, doing everything except letting a boy put his cock inside me. He could finger me all he wanted because I was a horny little thing and it felt fucking amazing, but I was terrified of getting pregnant, so no cocks allowed, even with a rubber.

My mom had me when she was sixteen, and she often reminded me how tough it was for her to be a young, single mom, at least until she met and married Earl, my stepfather when she was eighteen and he was thirty-one.

So, I'd let a boy stick his cock in my mouth, come in my hand, and, if I really liked him, slide it into my ass; but my pussy was off limits.

I guess I was considered the school slut because I made no bones about being sexually active, though I was very particular about who I fooled around with.

I lost my virginity my senior year to a transfer student from Mexico City named Greg Rivera. It didn't occur to me at the time why I was willing to let Greg pop my cherry when I wouldn't let other boys get close. I mean, I had been with much hotter guys that I wouldn't let fuck me. There was just something about Greg that made my nipples tingle and my water works gush like a river.

He was brooding and dark, with hair as black as a crow's wings and eyes black as night. He picked me up in his dad's work truck and we drove to the lake and fucked like rabbits on a blanket in the bed of the truck. Greg was a rough lover who didn't know the meaning of the words "take your time". He hadn't learned to be tender, so my cunt was sore the next day and my popped cherry hurt like a bitch, but I never regretted letting Greg be my first.

We screwed every chance we got over that summer. We taught each other to be unselfish lovers. I told him exactly what I liked and he told me exactly what he liked. We experimented and learned together. And neither of us ever walked away unsatisfied.

Greg had a summer job at the FoodMart and would steal condoms by the box from the pharmacy. I loved having him inside me, but I still wasn't willing to chance having a baby in there.

It wasn't until my mom saw Greg working at the grocery store that I understood why I'd let him be the one to pop my cherry. He was bagging groceries two lanes over and we were pretending not to know one another. Mom noticed him immediately, though she had no idea that we were sleeping together.

"He looks like your dad when I first met him," she said quietly, giving Greg a long look that I thought was a little creepy.

"He does?" I said with a frown. I squinted at Greg and felt the juices pooling in my panties. "I don't see it."

"When we get home look at that picture of your dad I gave you last year," she said. "You'll see."

The picture she was referring to was the only photograph I had of my bio-dad; the boy who had knocked her up with she was just fifteen. She only knew him as Jose, the son of a migrant farmworker picking oranges on my grandfather's farm. He was seventeen when the photo was taken, standing in front of an orange wagon next to my mom, then a gangly girl with pigtails and bony knees that she parted for him. Once the oranges were picked, Jose and his family moved on and my mom never saw him again.

She caught Greg and I looking at each other. She narrowed her eyes at me and shook her head. "Be careful, Courtney. Don't do what I did."

The next day, I was put on birth control and getting a lecture about sex from a woman who could have been taking lessons from me.

She was right about one thing: Greg could have been my father's clone. I stared at the fifteen-year-old photograph with my mouth hanging open. The resemblance was uncanny. For a moment, I worried that we might have the same dad, but when I showed Greg the photo and voiced my fears, he just laughed and assured me his dad was fifty-eight and named Mario.

My friend Felicia, whose mom was a therapist, said I had a daddy complex. She said I gave up my cherry to Greg because he reminded me of my dad.

"That's the dumbest thing I've ever heard," I said. "And just gross."

"It's not that you wanted to fuck your own father, idiot," she explained, rolling her eyes. "It's that not having him around has left some kind of void in your brain that you filled with Greg, a boy who looks just like him."

"Ah, okay..." It sounded like a good theory, but what the fuck does a sixteen-year-old know about such things. All I know is that I never had sex with Greg again. I wouldn't even let him touch me. Every time I looked at him I thought of my dad.

It wasn't until I started college and began fucking men much older than me that my daddy complex really became apparent.

I no longer fucked dark Mexican men who looked like my dad.

I only fucked men old enough to be my dad.

Men like Logan Clark.

CHAPTER THREE: Logan Clark

I dug my fingers into Martha's fleshy hips and held my breath so I didn't cum too quickly this time. The last time we fucked we were both shitfaced after the monthly faculty dinner and had sex in the backseat of her Volvo in the parking lot of Ruby Tuesdays.

I normally don't cum that quickly; not since high school. The mistake I made was letting her suck my cock too long in the lady's bathroom. By the time we got to her car, and she pulled up her skirt and peeled off her pantyhose and panties, I was already ready to explode.

She wiggled herself backward onto my cock and slid her hips back and forth a couple of times and that was all she wrote. I shot my load before I even knew what was happening.

Luckily for her and me, I was able to hold the hard-on long enough for her to get her rocks off. There's nothing more embarrassing to a guy than shooting his load too quickly, especially with a woman like Martha Warner, who would have never let me forget such a fucking faux pas.

Martha could be a ball-busting bitch. She already gave me shit about enough stuff. I didn't need to add premature ejaculation to the list.

This time things had gone much smoother because she didn't have the chance to blow me in the restaurant bathroom. After the monthly faculty dinner, she invited me to her place for a nightcap. Okay, that's not exactly how she put it. It was more like, "Professor Clark, I want you to come back to my place and fuck me till my knees buckle."

It wasn't an invitation. It was a command. And since she was the Dean at Golden State and held the keys to my future, I readily complied. I would be eligible for tenure in a few months, which would give me the job for life. If I had to fuck an attractive fifty-year-old divorcee to make that happen, it was a small price to pay.

We managed to make it just inside the door of the huge Victorian house the university provided her with before tearing each other's clothes off.

Martha was ravenous, nearly ripping the buttons off my shirt as she tore it open and literally jerking me around as she tried to unbuckle my belt. I pushed her hard against the wall and pressed my lips to hers as I peeled off her white silk blouse and unhooked the bra that held her huge tits. Her tits came free with a bounce. They hung low on her chest, but were still full and firm and sported the largest nipples I'd ever had the pleasure of sucking.

Martha grabbed my cock and moaned in my ear when she found it long, hard and ready. She tugged at it as I unzipped her skirt and pushed it down her ample thighs. I was a little surprised to find that she was not wearing her usual pantyhose and granny panties. Smart planning on her part. She knew where we'd end up before she even left her house that day. And she didn't want to slow me down.

My hand went between her legs. Her bush was thick and curly, her cunt hot and dripping. When my fingers slid over her clit and across her folds, she tightened her grip on my cock and commanded me to follow her into the bedroom.

"I want to watch you fuck me," she said, still holding my cock to lead me into her master bathroom. The bathroom had a long vanity and a long mirror on the wall above it. She leaned forward to brace her palms on the vanity and stuck out her big ass. Her bulbous tits hung swung from her chest.

"Fuck me from behind, Logan," she said, wiggling her ass. "So I can watch you fuck me."

"Yes, ma'am," I said, smiling at her in the mirror. I put my hands on her hips and positioned myself behind her. I took my cock in my hand and guided the purple head between her legs. Martha's juices were flowing like a river. Her pussy was already drenched, filling the room with the tangy scent of her juices.

I swirled the head of my cock around her hole to lube it up, then rocked my hips forward and, with one thrust, impaled my cock fully into her. Martha didn't have the tightest pussy I'd ever fucked, but she could take almost all of my ten-inch cock and not bat an eye.

I dug my fingers into her fleshy hips and looked down to watch my long cock sliding in and out of her cunt. I moved my hands to her ass and kneaded her ass cheeks. She moaned louder when the tip of my finger probed her asshole.

"Yes... Logan... oh yes..." Her voice came in gusts, pushed out of her as my cock pummeled in and out of her.

I glanced at the two of us in the mirror. Martha had her eyes closed. Her round cheeks were rosy red. Her forehead was sweaty. Her mouth was hanging open. Her tongue hung over her bottom lip. She was panting like a dog.

Martha wasn't really my type, but that hadn't stopped me from fucking her on occasion for the last few months. She was in her early fifties, short, chunky, with auburn hair that always showed a hint of gray roots and more wrinkles from frowning than smiling.

She might have been my type twenty years and thirty pounds ago like Sheila Denning was now. Sheila was the smoking hot head of the Math Department who I was also fucking on a sporadic basis. Sheila was married to Chuck Denning, Golden State's head football coach. We fucked when he was at away games. Still, I had to admit, Martha's cunt was just fine for her age and her tits were humongous, so I couldn't complain.

I'd gotten more pussy since taking the job at Golden State than I'd ever gotten in my life before, and most of it came from my fellow professors and administrators, ladies like Martha and Sheila; some younger, some older, some thinner, some chunkier, all horny and willing to do whatever the fuck I told them to do.

I guess the word had gotten around the staff.

If you're a lonely lady with a tight pussy and a bottle of Jack Daniels, Logan Clark was your man. And your pussy didn't have to be that tight, so long as you had the booze.

"Oh... Logan... I'm cumming..." Martha moaned, leaning up on her hands with her ass still out for me. She took her big jugs in her palms and kneaded them until she left red marks. Her nipples were the size of my thumbs. I licked my lips as I watched her squeezed them until they turned dark red.

I was ready to cum with her. I put my hands back on her hips and tightened every muscle in my body to summon my orgasm. As Martha lifted her head and screamed my name, I filled her pussy with my hot milk and she gushed tangy juice all over my balls. Two more good thrusts all the way in and she begged me to stop.

I opened my eyes to find her smiling at me in the mirror. She blew a strand of hair from her forehead and puckered her lips at me. "You're amazing, Professor Clark," she cooed. "I'm so glad you came to Golden State."

"You're not bad yourself, Dean Warner," I said, wiggling my hips and giving her ass a playful slap. I stepped back to let my cock slide out of her and reached in to turn on the shower.

I held out a hand to her.

"Come on. I made a mess on you. Let me clean you up."

CHAPTER FOUR: Logan

It was nearly midnight by the time I managed to pry myself from between Martha's ample thighs and escape into the night. Martha was a nice lady and a decent fuck, but like so many other women her age, she was needy; clingy and codependent. I'd never know why I couldn't just fuck a woman and go home instead of having to cuddle and make small talk.

Why can't I just say, "Hey, thanks for the pussy. See ya!"

Martha stood in her front door in her bathrobe, waving as I climbed onto my motorcycle and sped away. I didn't even bother with the helmet. That would have taken too much time. I just wanted to get the fuck out of there before Martha asked me to spend the night.

I rented a one bedroom bungalow just off campus. It wasn't much, but the rent was cheap and the commute to work was short. I aimed my motorcycle in that direction and opened the throttle, putting as much distance behind me and Dean Martha Warner as fast as I could.

I had to stop at a red light as I cruised through the center of town. I took the time to blow out a long breath and glance at my watch. It was twelve-thirty, but I was too keyed-up to sleep and not ready to call it a night, so when I saw the sign for Goldie's, the dive bar where the students and "cool" professors hung out, a hundred yards ahead, I decided to stop for a nightcap. With any luck my pal Tom Brooks would be there drowning his sorrows and willing to buy drinks in exchange for a shoulder to cry on.

Tom was three months out of a bad divorce and my best friend on campus. He was about my age, a little shorter and heavier, and was the head of the Marketing Department.

We became drinking buddies the night he showed up at Goldie's to get drunk after walking in on his wife getting fucked in the ass in his bed by a very large, black, Golden State football player by the name of Desean Golf.

I'll never forget the first-time Tom told the tale. "I opened the door and the kid just looked at me and said, 'Hey, man. Wassup?'. He never stopped fucking her and she didn't say a word. I mean, who does that?"

I remembered giving him a sympathetic look and saying something stupid like, "Kids these days. Go figure. Come on, let's get drunk."

That's what I was doing the night Tom came in, getting drunk, because that's what I do.

I teach.

I fuck.

I drink.

Rinse and repeat.

It's a pretty routine life.

It was Friday night and Goldie's lot was full. There were kids milling around the parking lot, sitting on the hoods of cars, drinking and smoking pot, even though the cops cruised by every few minutes. The cops liked the money that came from having a state university in their little city, so unless the kids were wreaking havoc or gangbanging hookers on the sidewalk, the cops always gave them a pass.

I smiled when I saw Tom's puke green Prius parked near the front door. That meant he'd been there drinking most of the night. He'd be good and drunk and buying drinks for coeds he wanted to fuck, but never would. Me, I could probably fuck a different coed every day if I didn't have my strict "no coed fucking" rule, but Tom wasn't me. He was dumpy and sad and pathetic. Even the ugly chicks stayed away from him. Maybe someday I'd take him under my wing and get him laid. It was the least that I could do given the amount of alcohol he'd bought me over the last few months.

I parked my bike at the end of the line and pushed my way through the front door. The place was dark, smoky, loud, and stank of cigarettes and old beer. I fucking loved it. I stood at the door for a moment, letting my eyes adjust to the darkness. I saw Tom sitting at one end of the bar, a beer mug and a shot glass in front of him. He waved when he saw me. His face lit up like a Christmas tree. His wingman had arrived.

"Hey, I didn't think I'd see you tonight," Tom said, his words slurring. He wrapped his arms around my neck and slobbered a kiss on my cheek. He waved down the bartender and ordered a round of beer and whiskey shots for us both.

"I'd never miss a chance to drink on your tab," I said, sliding onto the stool next to him. I glanced over my shoulder. There was a bad four-piece band on a homemade stage in the corner, murdering a Bob Segar song. The small dance floor was shoulder-to-shoulder with kids writhing and sweating like pigs. Every table was taken and the bar was backed up three-deep on the other end. Just another night at Goldie's.

"So, how is Dean Warner," he asked with a sly smile. "I saw you two leave the faculty dinner together."

"She's actually pretty fucking good," I said, nodding with the shot glass at my lips. "In fact, she asked about you tonight. I think she's on the hunt for fresh blood."

Tom blinked at me, then scowled. "Fuck you, she did not."

"She did, too," I said, grinning through the lie. "I said 'Martha, you should fuck my good pal, Tom'. And she said, 'Tell him to make a fucking appointment', no pun intended."

"You're an asshole," he said, shooting back the whiskey and wiping his mouth on the back of his hand.

"You should fuck her, Tommy boy," I said, seriously now, licking the whiskey from my lips. "You would not be disappointed. It would do you a world of good to get a little fresh stink on your dick."

"She doesn't want to fuck me," he slurred, rolling his eyes. "Does she?"

"She might," I said, giving him a shrug with my eyes. "I'd be happy to hook you up."

"I don't know," he said. His eyes were red and his head wobbled a little. "I'm still..."

"I know, you're still pining away over your football-player-fucking ex-wife," I said, shaking my head at him. "But Jesus, Tom, it's time to let go. She's gone. She's moved on. She already has another man."

"I know, I know," he said sadly, turning his head so I couldn't see him wipe his eyes. "I'll get back in the saddle someday."

"I think Martha Warner might actually have a saddle." I took a long pull from the beer mug and smacked my lips at him. "I know for a fact she likes being rode hard."

"You'd better be careful, my friend," Tom said, shaking his head. "You've slept with half the women on the faculty. Someday that legendary cock of yours is going to land you in serious trouble."

I leaned an elbow on the bar and snorted a laugh. "There are rules against fucking students," I said, flexing my eyebrows. "There are no such rules about fucking the esteemed female members of the faculty."

"There may not be rules," he said, waving his empty shot glass at the bartender. "But when you're fucking a bunch of women who work together and eat lunch in the cafeteria together every day, once they start comparing notes and figure out that you're screwing them all... then they go to report you to the dean and find out you're fucking her, too?" He drained the mug and shook his head. "You'll be lucky to get a job teaching at an online college in the middle of fucking Idaho."

I clutched my hands to my chest like an innocent man accused of horrible crimes. "I am but a vessel serving a hungry audience, Tom," I said. "You're a marketing professor. You should understand market supply and demand."

"I understand that most of the women you're fucking also have husbands who will cut your balls off if they catch you," he said. "And when that happens, don't come running to me because I'll just say I told you so."

"Can you run with your balls cut off?" I asked with a grin.

"I wouldn't know," he said with a sigh. "My ex got my balls in the settlement. I think she keeps them in a cigar box under her bed so she and whomever she is fucking at that moment can make fun of me."

"Jesus, man, you have to move on," I said.

"I'm trying," he said quietly. The bartender delivered another round and I picked up the shot glass and held it out to him.

"Here's to your ex, Tom," I toasted, tapping my glass to his. "May her pussy rot away and her tits fall off."

"That's awful," he said with a smirk.

"I know. Bottoms up, motherfucker."

We both shot back the whiskey and sighed. I put a hand on his shoulder and gave it a shake. "Come on, let's get you laid."

I leaned back with my elbows braced on the bar so I could survey the crowd. Tom and I were old enough to have fathered most of the kids there. I narrowed my eyes to scan the room, hoping to spot a table of older females who had stumbled in for a girl's night out and might be open to having their pipes cleaned by me and my pitiful friend.

There were probably a hundred kids in the club: drinking, dancing, acting like fools. They were young and good looking and having the time of their life. They didn't have a care in the world. They had their whole lives ahead of them. And I hated them all because they had the one thing I no longer had: a future full of promise and potential.

With enough drive and determination, they could do anything their hearts desired at this point in their lives, but most of them were too stupid to realize it and would squander their lives away.

Many of them would graduate soon and move onto grad school or mundane jobs where they'd labor for the next forty or fifty years and pray they would have enough money to live on once they retired.

They'd get married to someone they would grow to hate; have kids who would grow to hate them, and would spend their days working their asses off to build a life rather than living life.

I knew all this because I had done it.

They say youth is wasted on the young.

I say youth is wasted on the ignorant.

If I knew twenty-five years ago what I know today, I wouldn't be standing in a dive bar in a shit college town, getting shitfaced drunk with a whiny bastard who will probably end up blowing his brains out some day, fucking my way through the aging female faculty of a second-rate state university.

I was a forty-two-year-old, twice divorced, borderline alcoholic who live in a one bedroom shithole on a salary that was less than I made when I came out of grad school twenty years ago. I lived for the booze and the pussy. At this point in my life, little else mattered.

CHAPTER FIVE: Logan

"Why the long face?" I heard a chipper, female voice say. I shook away the darkness of my thoughts and turned to see a beautiful girl with fiery red hair cascading over her shoulders and blue eyes standing next to me at the bar. There was an empty beer mug on the bar in front of her. She was glancing sideways at me, smiling, waiting for the bartender to bring her a fresh mug of beer.

"Do I have a long face?" I asked, arching my eyebrows.

"Well, not anymore," she said, smiling with her eyes.

I turned to look at her as the bartender slid a full mug between her hands. I let my eyes drift down her body. She was wearing a tight tank-top that strained against her big tits and stopped an inch above her belly button. She was wearing denim cutoffs and sandals. She had a nice round ass; a bubble butt, the kids called it. The shorts were low cut on her hips. I could see the top of a red thong and the hint of dimples above her luscious ass cheeks. She caught me looking and smiled again.

"See anything you like?" she asked.

I glanced around at Tom, who was staring back at me with a look of fear in his wide eyes, slowly shaking his head. He leaned in and whispered, "She's a student. She's off limits."

I whispered back. "I know. I'm gonna see if her mom is here. I told you I was gonna get you laid."

"You're such a fucking asshole," he said, picking up a napkin to wipe the foam off his lips. He wadded up the napkin and threw it at the bar. "I'm gonna take a leak. Order us another round."

"Roger that," I said like a good wingman. I watched him stumble through the crowd for a moment, then turned back to the hot redhead with the big tits. She had her elbows and tits resting on the bar. She was casually sipping her beer and watching ESPN on the TV behind the bar.

Was she waiting for me to hit on her, I wondered. If so, she was going to have a long wait. I didn't fuck students. No matter how incredibly hot and seductive they were. I needed this job too much. It was all that I had left. No pussy was worth risking it. Even one that I was sure would taste as sweet as hers.

I picked up my beer and leaned my elbows on the bar like her. I pretended to watch TV, but couldn't resist checking her out from the corner of my eye. She looked familiar. It took a moment, but I recognized her from my advanced accounting class. Candy something or other... No, Courtney... Courtney Shaw...

She was probably the smartest girl in the class.

Definitely, the hottest.

She usually kept her mane of red hair pulled back into a tight ponytail and never wore makeup because, well, why would she? She always sat three rows back in the center, and sometimes asked questions that she probably already knew the answers to. I'd been teaching hot coeds long enough to know all their tricks. She wanted me to notice her, which just made me ignore her all the more. I'm a man of willpower, but a girl like her could probably wear me down if given the chance. I knew she'd probably be amazing in bed and my cock did a little twitch at the thought of it, but I had my hands full juggling the five or six mature women I was fucking. I didn't need to complicate things by working my way through the hot girls in my class.

"I've seen you here before," she said, talking to me, but keeping her eyes on the television. "Always with your sad friend, Professor Brooks."

"How do you know my friend is sad?" I asked.

"The whole school knows that he walked in on his wife getting banged in the ass by that football player," she said, letting her bare shoulders go up and down. "He comes in here every night and starts drinking early, then you show up after whatever it is you do to drive him home." She turned to face me with one elbow on the bar and the mug of beer in her hand. "My question has always been, what is it that you do before you arrive here, Professor Clark? Always with your shirt misbuttoned and your hair all a mess."

I frowned as I glanced down at the front of my shirt. It was not misbuttoned. "My shirts not..."

She smiled and tapped a fingernail to my chin. "No, but I made you look," she said.

She took a long pull from the mug and licked the foam from her lips. My eyes followed the trail her tongue left on her lips. She slid in a step closer. Her fingers toyed with a button on my shirt.

"What are you doing?" I asked, staring into her eyes. I didn't step back. I should have, but I didn't. My brain was screaming at me to move, but my cock was telling my feet to stand their ground.

She leaned in and whispered in my ear.

"I want to suck your cock, Professor Clark. And no one would ever have to know."

She stepped back, drank the last of her beer, and set the mug on the bar. Before she walked away, she gave me a dreamy look and licked her lips.

"I'm going to pee," she said. "Why don't you join me."

CHAPTER SIX: Courtney

I saw Logan Clark the moment he came through Goldie's front door. I'd been sitting at the corner table with my roommate Mindy and a few other friends for nearly two hours, sipping slowly on a Diet Coke to stay sober while hoping he'd show up.

I had spotted Professor Brooks at the bar when I came in. He was already slumped on his usual stool, drowning his sorrows in beer and whiskey shots.

Poor guy.

Everyone knew that he'd caught his wife banging a football player a few months back and still wasn't over it. Since then, he was in Goldie's every night, always at the end of the bar, always drunk and sad and whining to anyone who would listen.

If my sights hadn't been set on nailing Logan Clark, I might have tossed poor Professor Brooks a pity-fuck, just to let him know what a young pussy felt like, and to let him know that he would be okay and could move on. There were lots of desperate old ladies on eHarmony that would have snapped him up.

Oh well, maybe Professor Clark would hook him up with one of the old bitches he was regularly banging once we started fucking. There was no doubt in my mind: once Logan Clark got a taste of what I had between my legs, he'd never want to fuck those old ladies again.

Golden State is a big school, but talk and innuendo run rampant like a small-town rumor mill. It was common knowledge that Logan Clark was fucking half the female faculty and would probably fuck the other half before all was said and done.

He seemed to be working his way through the entire academic staff. Rumor was that he was even fucking old Dean Martha Warner. If so, I bet he had to brush away the cobwebs and blow away the dust off her old cooch before shoving his big cock into her. Christ, it had to be like fucking a dry hole. I had no idea what he was thinking. Why is he screwing those old bags when he could have his pick of hot, young coeds... like me.

Maybe he was just afraid of losing his job. There were strict rules prohibiting fraternization, i.e. sex of any kind, between professors and students, but I guess the professors and administrators could fuck each other till the cows came home.

I couldn't think of any other reason a man like Logan Clark, who could pass for thirty any day of the week, would want to shove his sweet cock into the dusty old bungholes of the faculty women.

The only woman he was fucking that was halfway decent was Sheila Denning, the head of the math department. She was probably my mom's age and was holding up pretty well. She had a cute face, good tits, and a decent ass that the male students always commented on. I'm sorry, the other women Logan was screwing were just old skanks.

Hmmm, maybe that was his thing.

I had a daddy complex.

Maybe Logan Clark had an old skank complex.

If so... ew!!

Logan finally came in after midnight and went straight to the bar to hang with Professor Brooks, who was so drunk by then he could barely stand. I gave Logan time to get a couple of shots in him, then picked up an empty beer mug from the table and pushed my way to the bar.

I bellied up to the bar next to Logan, expecting him to notice me right off the bat. I had on a super-tight crop top and a pair of short denims that showed off my tan, toned legs. Logan was oblivious. He was staring off into space with a sour look on his face, like he was thinking about something he didn't like.

I waited for a second, then cleared my throat and said, "Why the long face?" When he looked at me and smiled I almost creamed my cut-offs.

Ten minutes later, I told him I wanted to suck his cock and strolled off toward the women's restroom. Now here I was, standing at the bathroom sink, glancing at my makeup in the mirror to kill time, waiting to hear him knock on the door.

Another two minutes went by.

Several girls knocked on the door and yelled that they had to pee, but I barked at them that the restroom was occupied.

I washed my hands and took my time drying them off.

Still, no Logan Clark.

Well, fuck.

So much for that idea.

Maybe I was too young and hot for him.

Maybe I didn't have enough wrinkles on my face or rust on my cunt.

Maybe my boobs were too young and firm for his tastes.

Maybe I'd been wrong to set my sights on Logan Clark.

Maybe I should drag Professor Brooks back to my place and work out my frustrations on him. He wasn't nearly as hot as Professor Clark, but he'd do in a horny pinch. He would be so grateful I bet he'd even let me use a strap-on on him.

Regardless, I wasn't giving up on my quest to have Logan Clark's cock inside every hole in my body.

I'd just have to adjust my strategy.

When the prey evades, the hunter adjusts.

Then I pulled open the restroom door and there he was, standing with his arms spread and hands on the doorframe, like Jesus on the cross, with a devious look in his eye. I glanced down at the front of his jeans to check out the bulge I'd been dying to see for so long. I was not disappointed

He put his hand between my breasts and pushed me back into the bathroom, then closed and locked the door.

When his dark eyes met mine and he started toward me, I felt my hot pussy juices starting to flow.

CHAPTER SEVEN: Logan

I stood at the bar for a few minutes, finishing my beer and letting my various body parts argue it out.

My brain argued that it wasn't worth risking tenure, even if it was just a blowjob in the restroom. My brain knew from experience that blowjobs in restrooms often led to other things, like fucking in the back of a Volvo.

My cock and balls joined together to call my brain a pussy and told my feet to get moving, goddammit.

My brain called my cock and balls troublemakers and told my feet not to move.

My tongue wondered what her pussy would taste like.

My lips wondered how long her nipples might be.

My brain told them all to shut the fuck up.

Then things turned ugly.

My cock threatened to piss in my pants if it didn't get its way.

"I think I've had enough," Tom said as he stumbled back from the restroom and slid onto the stool. He frowned at the full mug of beer and the fresh whiskey shot waiting for him. "Did I order that?"

"You did," I said, patting him on the back. "Drink up. I'm gonna take a piss, then I'll get you home."

My cock and balls whistled a happy tune as my feet walked us toward the restrooms at the back of the club.

My lips and tongue joined in, humming along.

Even my fingers gave a little snap.

Only my brain was silent.

It was smart enough to know when it had lost an argument.

And loved to say I told you so.

* * *

The restroom door opened just as I was about to knock. Courtney Shaw gawked at me with a shocked look on her face, as if she was surprised to see me, like maybe she didn't think I'd call her bluff.

I put a hand between her big tits and pushed her back into the restroom. I closed and locked the door. I licked my lips and moved toward her before my brain had time to change its mind.

She was standing with her back against the wall. I stepped in front of her and pressed my body to hers. My cock pulsed against her. I kept my hands at my side. My nostrils flared as I breathed in her scent; soapy, sweaty, tangy sex.

"You said something about sucking my cock," I said, my eyes sweeping around her beautiful face. She put her fingers on my belt buckle and leaned her lips up to mine. I pushed her hands away and shook my head. I put my hands on her shoulders and pushed her hard against the wall. She blinked at me with a look of fear in her eyes.

I said, "No kissing. No touching. No talking. Just sucking. And swallowing."

She frowned and let her eyes burn into mine for a second, then a smile slowly curled at the corners of her plump lips. I fought the urge to kiss her, to suck on her tongue and dig my fingers into her big tits. I wanted to bend her over the sink and fuck her hard from behind, but I couldn't allow that to happen. That was a line I could not cross.

Just a blowjob, my brain said in a scolding tone, like a mother telling her unruly kids they only got one scoop of ice cream because they've been so bad. *Take out your cock, shove it in her mouth, and let her suck you off, then get the fuck out of here before someone sees you together.*

"Fine," she said, swirling her tongue over her lips. "No kissing. No touching. No talking. Just sucking and swallowing." She pushed me back and nodded at the bulge pushing against the front of my jeans. "But I can't do anything until you whip it out."

I gave her a blank look as I unbuckled my belt, undid my jeans, and pushed them down to my knees. My cock sprang out like a diving board, hard and long. It was so motherfucking hard it ached in anticipation of having her lips around it.

"Suck it," I whispered, leaning back against the sink. She got to her knees in front of me. Her fingers came up to go around my shaft.

"No touching," I said again, pushing her hand away. "Only your mouth."

"Professor Clark, so many rules," she said, looking up at me with a smile. She held up her hand. "I can't just use one hand to hold it steady?"

"You said you wanted to suck my cock," I said. "Now shut the fuck up and suck it."

She put her hands behind her back and leaned in until her lips were an inch from the head of my cock. She put the tip of her tongue to the tip of my cock and swirled it around the head, making me jump.

She stuck out her tongue as far as it would go and dipped her head to lift up my cock and lick the bottom of my shaft from my balls to the slit. I shuddered as her tongue paused to lick the little bundle of nerves at the base of the head.

I put my hands behind me and braced my palms on the sink as she took me into her mouth, pressing her lips around the shaft and leaning forward until the head of my cock hit the back of her throat.

She was good. Better even than Sheila Denning, who gave the best blowjobs on campus, at least to me. Courtney didn't gag, even though she had nine inches of cock in her mouth and throat.

I bit my tongue and forced myself not to moan out loud. I'd been with a lot of women, but I'd never had a blowjob quite like this. I tried to remember the last time I'd been with a twenty-something year old. Sadly, I couldn't remember, it had been that long.

Courtney slid her mouth over my cock until her nose was nearly touching my curly blond pubes, then she tightened her lips around the shaft and drew her mouth back slowly until the head of my cock appeared at her lips.

"Holy... fuck..." I sighed, swallowing hard, trying to keep my knees from shaking.

"Do you like that, professor?" she said, smiling up at me. "You should feel what I can do with my pussy."

"No talking," I said, the words panting out of me. "Suck me. Make me cum, swallow it all."

"With pleasure," she said, taking me into her mouth again. I closed my eyes as she quickened the pace of her suction, my cock sliding in and out faster now, her lips wrapping tighter, milking me with each incredible stroke.

I began to moan, which made her moan and suck even faster. I could feel the orgasm building in my balls. Every muscle in my body tightened and I held my breath as I exploded in her mouth.

I heard her moan and looked down to see milky white ropes of cum shooting into her open mouth and down her chin. She couldn't resist bringing a hand up to milk my cock as it shot its load. I didn't stop her. It felt too fucking amazing.

I blew out a long breath as she squeezed my cock one last time to get out every last drop of hot jizz. She licked my cock clean and leaned back on her heels. She wiped her mouth on the back of her hand, looked up at me, and smiled.

"Are you sure you don't want to continue this at my place?" she asked. She put her hands on the sides of her big tits and squeezed them together. "If you have some silly rule about not fucking your students, you can stick your cock between my tits and come on my chest. Or in my ass..."

Wow, who was this girl and where had she been all my life?

Oh yeah, she's been in middle school.

I tucked my cock, still damp with her spit, back into my pants, then reached down to lift her up. She was momentarily in my arms. She pressed herself against me. Her lips were close enough to mine that I could smell my cum on her breath.

I fought to resist the urge to kiss her, to grab her ass and pull her into me. Thankfully, Tom pounded on the door, interrupting what might have been a very bad decision on my part.

"Hey, Logan, you in there?" he called, words slurring. He slapped a palm on the door. "Come on, man, it's time to go home."

"I have to go," I said, gazing into her eyes.

"I know," she said, dragging a fingernail down my chin. She pulled away from me and smiled. "I'll see you in class."

CHAPTER EIGHT: Courtney

"So, I gave him the best blowjob of his life, then he casually tucked his cock back into his jeans and ducked out the door like it was no big deal. I mean, seriously? Is that how he acts when old Martha Warner is blowing him in the restroom at Ruby Tuesdays?"

Mindy was sitting cross-legged on the foot of my bed, digging into the tub of mint chocolate chip ice cream sitting between us and listening to me rant about my encounter with Logan Clark in Goldie's restroom. She held the spoon between her lips and gawked at me.

"What? Dean Warner gave him a blowjob in the restroom at Ruby Tuesdays? No fucking way."

"Way," I said, dipping my spoon into the tub.

"Wait, how do you know that?"

I rolled my eyes with the spoon at my mouth. Licking ice cream from my lips, I said, "Let's just say that a certain professor that has a crush on me told me about it. It was after a faculty dinner or something. He said Warner was drunk and practically dragged Logan into the women's restroom, gave him a blowjob, then fucked him in the back of her car."

"No fucking way," Mindy said again. It was her favorite saying. "Honestly, Courtney, I don't understand why you're so hot for this guy. I mean, he's a total pussy hound and seems more interested in old ladies than young girls. You could fuck any other professor on staff. Why are you so hung up on Logan Clark?"

"There's just something about him that makes my blood boil," I said, licking ice cream off the spoon. "Like tonight, I'm on my knees in the fucking restroom with his cock in my mouth, and all I could think about was how happy I was making *him*. I kept looking up at his face and it just made me want to do anything to please him."

"Oh my god, Courtney," she said, eyes wide. "This isn't just another old guy you want to fuck. You've got a major crush on him."

"No, I don't," I argued. "And he's not an old guy."

"Yes you do and yes he is," she said, shaking the spoon at me. "I've known you for three years and I know how you operate."

I frowned at her. "What does that mean?"

"It means you're a borderline nympho with a major daddy complex," she said, trying to be all serious and analytical through the haze of alcohol, pot, and ice cream that was running through her system. "You've fucked a lot of guys, but you've never had that dreamy look in your eye when you talked about them."

"What dreamy look," I said, struggling to put on a blank face. "I'm just drunk."

"Bullshit," she snorted. "You nursed a Diet Coke all fucking night and you watched the door like a fucking sniper, waiting for him to come in."

"What, are you monitoring me now?" I asked, seriously getting a little pissed.

"No, I'm just telling you what I saw." She dug out another spoonful of ice cream and put it between her lips. With the ice cream melting on her tongue, she said, "I think you might have a thing for Logan Clark that goes beyond your usual infatuation."

I thought about it for a moment, then stuck my spoon into the ice cream and gave her a little shrug. "So, what if I do?"

"You tell me," she said, picking up the tub of ice cream and swinging her legs over the side of the bed. "What if you do?"

* * *

I waited until Mindy left and closed my door, then I leaned down to reach beneath my bed and bring up my Magic Toy Box.

My Magic Toy Box was what I called the shoe box that held my personal collection of toys: dildos, vibrators, ben-wa balls, butt plugs, and other goodies I had collected over the years of my sexual misadventures. Sucking Logan's cock had left me hot and horny. There was no way I was going to be able to sleep until I gave myself a little satisfaction.

I chose the aptly-named Vibrating Egg; a small vibrator the shape and size of an egg, designed to be turned on and shoved deep inside the cunt. I swear, you can feel the damn thing vibrating your pussy walls all the way into your throat.

Then I chose a twelve-inch rubber dildo that felt incredibly like the real thing. I tugged my nightshirt over my head and tossed it aside. I never wore panties when I slept.

I set the Magic Toy Box on the floor and turned off the light, then lay back and spread my legs.

I turned on the Vibrating Egg. My pussy flushed at the sound of it. I inserted it into my cunt and pushed it in as far as it would go. My entire body began to tingle as it was vibrated from the inside out.

I didn't have to lube up the dildo because my pussy had been gushing since the moment Logan came across my lips. I exhaled as I slid the dildo into my pussy. When the head of the dildo hit the Vibrating Egg, the vibrations went thru the dildo and into my clit. I held it there for a moment, shuddering, then began sliding the dildo in and out, in and out.

I reached down with my left hand to dip my fingers into my pussy, coating them with my own juicy lube. I rolled the fingers over my clit and moaned at the sensation. My nipples plumped like thimbles on my breasts. My mouth was suddenly dry. I licked my lips and closed my eyes.

Logan Clark magically appeared in my mind's eye.

He was on top of me, all blond hair and thick muscles, his long cock buried deep inside me.

He leaned down to gently kiss my lips.

Now, here is where it pays to be dexterous, like being able to pat your head and rub your belly at the same time.

As the Vibrating Egg sent quaking shivers through my pussy walls and into my body, I fucked myself hard with the dildo while rubbing my clit. Someday I'll have to video the scene because I probably looked like a circus act, but I didn't care. If I'd had nipple clamps, all of my bases would have been covered.

Note to self: buy nipple clamps...

I could feel the orgasm coming on. My muscles tensed. I could feel the vibrations from the Egg in my throat. My pussy lips clung to the slick dildo as it pummeled into me. My clit was swollen and raw. I curled my toes and bit my lip.

When the orgasm erupted, I shoved the dildo in as far as it would go and clenched my pussy muscles around it. In my imagination, it was Logan Clark' cock deep inside me. It was his fingers on my clit. His tongue on my nipples and in my mouth.

I came so hard my body literally spasmed for a full minute afterward, as if it was having to throw itself back into sync after being vibrated to another dimension.

I blew out a long breath and let the dildo and Egg slide out of my cunt on their own.

I switched off the Egg and put it back into my Magic Toy Box along with the dildo. I'd clean them both off tomorrow.

My pussy and ass were drenched. The aroma of my tangy juices hung in the air. There was a huge wet spot on the sheet beneath me. I picked up the nightshirt to dry myself off, then rolled over with Logan Clark still on my mind.

Tomorrow was a new day.

I was not giving up on him yet.

I had two weeks before the end of the semester.

That was plenty of time to make my fantasies come true.

CHAPTER NINE: Logan

Monday morning; I was standing at the blackboard, writing out the formula for determining the deductibility of a business expense for my next class, when Tom Brooks stuck his head in the door.

He looked like shit. His eyes were bloodshot, his clothes disheveled, his hair a mess. The only good thing about him was that he was carrying two tall cups of Starbucks coffee.

"Wow, Tom, you look like shit," I said, dusting chalk off my hands to accept the cup of coffee. "Are you okay?" I pried off the lid and took the coffee to my desk. I sat down and motioned him to a seat.

"Thanks, buddy," he said, stifling a yawn with the back of his hand. "I went back to Goldie's last night to watch the football game. Got a little drunk."

"Man, you have got to ease off on the booze," I said seriously. I swept my eyes around his face for a moment. His bloodshot eyes and slack jaw reminded me of a bloodhound. I could see tiny blood vessels mapping the skin beneath his eyes and across his nose. Tom was getting the marks of a drunk, all because his fucking wife cheated on him and left him.

"I'm fine," he said, prying the lid off his cup and blowing into the steaming coffee before taking a careful sip. "I thought I'd see you there last night. Where were you?"

I shook my head. "I needed a weekend getaway," I said. "I rode my motorcycle into the mountains for the day. Didn't get back until late last night."

"Wow, that sounds nice," he said with a wistful sigh. "Wendy never would let me have a motorcycle."

"Wendy's fucking gone, Tom," I said, huffing at him. "Go buy yourself a bike. Next time I go on a day trek, you can come with me."

He made a sour face and let his round shoulders go up and down. "Nah, I'd just kill myself."

"Like you're killing yourself with the booze?" I asked.

He scoffed and shook his head. "What? I'm not killing myself with the booze. Where is this coming from? I thought you understood."

"Understood what?" I arched my eyebrows over the cup, waiting for him to answer.

"That I'm in pain," he snapped, blinking back tears. He wiggled a finger at me. "You don't understand, Logan. You don't know what it's like to have your heart ripped out and stomped into the ground by someone you love."

"Don't I?" I took a deep breath and shook my head slowly. "Tom, I've been married and divorced twice. Do you think I wanted to get divorced either of those times?"

"Well, I just assumed... I mean... You're so good with women..."

"My first wife was named Darby," I said. "Beautiful girl, blonde hair, blue eyes, killer body, great sense of humor. We dated three years and got married right out of college. It took her less six months to find a guy she loved more than me. I came home one day to our ratty little apartment and she was just gone. She left me a note that said that I didn't make her happy, so she was moving on. I didn't make her happy, like that was my job or something."

"At least you didn't walk in on her having anal sex with a three-hundred-pound black kid," he said.

"There is that," I said, nodding.

"What about wife number two?"

"That would be Tracy, who came along a few years later. She was a knockout brunette, younger than me, big tits, nice ass, could suck the fuzz off a tennis ball. She was my teaching assistant at NYU. We got married in June and she kicked me to the curb in September. Seems she just woke up one day and realized that I wasn't the guy she wanted me to be. When I came home that day, she'd packed all my shit in boxes and left it on the front lawn."

"Jesus, Logan, I had no idea..." He gave me a pitiful look. "Did you love them? Were you devastated?"

I shrugged. "I thought I did and I probably was. I started drinking, feeling sorry for myself, staying out all night, missing work, fucking any woman who would let me between her legs. I became a sad drunk, Tom, just like you."

He blinked at the insult, but didn't say a word.

"I drank at night, I drank at lunch, I drank in class, I drank before class... One day my students found me passed out at my desk at ten in the morning. They called the dean and she called 911. I had almost killed myself. Alcohol poisoning. I'd been drinking for three days straight. They took me to a detox center and dried me out for thirty days."

"Damn," he said, staring down into his coffee cup. I hoped he understood that he was headed down the same dark path I had been on. I hated it for him. He was too good a guy to ruin his life because his wife was a cunt. He was a much better guy than I was. I could only hope that he realized that before it was too late.

"Anyway, I decided that I had to get out of New York City, so I managed to land this job four years ago. And if I don't fuck things up, I'll be eligible for tenure in the three months."

He nodded as he listened. Quietly, he said, "So, when your wives left you, did you think it was your fault?"

"For a long time, I did," I said with a long sigh. "They both blamed me, said I wasn't the man they thought I was. I thought about that long and hard while I was in detox."

"And what conclusion did you reach?" he asked.

"That I was just me," I said, smiling through a long sigh. "I had always been just me, but they wanted me to be someone else, someone that they could change and mold to fit their needs."

"So it wasn't your fault that they left?" he asked hopefully, as if looking for validation for the demise of his own shitty marriage.

"Oh, I'm sure it was my fault to some degree," I said with a shrug. "I was no saint, but I think they left because they couldn't change me into the man they wanted me to be. Once I understood that, I also understood that it was their fault as much as mine because they had both married a guy they thought they could change to fit their idea of what the perfect man was. Leaving me was them accepting the fact that they had fucked up, not me." I cut him a grin. "At least that's what a psyche professor I slept with told me."

"Wendy said she fucked that football player because I no longer satisfied her," he said, a faraway look in his eye. "She said it was all my fault."

"Tom, Wendy was a selfish cunt who fucked a football player because she wanted to, not because you drove her to it," I said, putting a hand on his shoulder and giving him a little shake. "Rather than wallow in pity and booze, you should thank the good lord that she's gone. Now you can find a woman who will appreciate you for you."

"You really think so," he said, rubbing a knuckle under his eyes. "I mean, find a good woman who will appreciate me for me?"

"I really do," I said with a nod. "But you have to dry out, man, because your body is going to start craving the booze, and when that happens, it's a lot harder to move on. You're heading down a very dark road that is a bitch to come back from. Trust me, I know."

"But you still drink," he said, narrowing his eyes at me. "Aren't you afraid that you'll fall off the wagon and head down that dark road again yourself?"

It was a good question without an easy answer. I didn't have time to explain the fucked-up, inner workings of my mind, so I just said, "It's all about moderation for me. When's the last time you saw me really drunk?"

His forehead furrowed in thought. "I don't think I've ever seen you really drunk."

"And you never will," I said. "I have a strict three drink rule. I take it as a personal challenge never to break my rule."

I was lying through my teeth to him, but it was a white lie told for his own good. I had fallen off the wagon so many times I couldn't count. I couldn't tell you how many times I'd gotten shitfaced and woke up in my car in a parking lot or in some stranger's bed. Or in my own bed with no idea how I made it home. Those were my demons to fight, not Tom's. He didn't need to hear the sordid details of my reality. He needed to deal with his own.

"So, you test yourself? You drink three drinks, then cut yourself off. You do it to prove to yourself that you can do it. That you're in control."

"Something like that," I said.

"Kind of like your rule about not fucking coeds," he said with a smile.

"Something like that."

"You have lots of rules, Logan."

I smiled. "I know. I've been told."

He shook his head and blew out his cheeks. "I'm not sure I have your willpower."

"Of course, you do," I said. "And you have me to help you."

"What does that mean?" He had a hopeful look in his eye.

"I want you to dry out for a week," I said. "No booze of any kind. And get back into the gym, start running again, concentrate on you and not Wendy."

"Okay, I can do that," he said, trying to smile. He gazed up from beneath his eyebrows. "And maybe I'll start dating again."

I chuckled and gave him a nod. "My friend, you go a week without booze and get some color back in your cheeks, and we will get you laid."

He smiled. "You promise."

"Scouts honor," I said, holding up three fingers. "Now get out of here. I have young minds to corrupt."

As he left the room, I glanced up at the clock. Students for my next class would be filtering in soon. Including Courtney Shaw, who had not left my thoughts since our restroom encounter two nights before.

I'd just bragged about my ability to resist temptation to Tom. I doubt he would have taken me seriously had he known that Courtney had given me a blowjob in Goldie's restroom.

I thought about that dark road again, the one I had stumbled down so many times before.

I closed my eyes, imagining it in my mind.

I saw Courtney Shaw standing in the middle of the dark road, holding out her hands, beckoning me to come along.

CHAPTER TEN: Courtney

Logan was sitting at his desk fiddling with his phone when I walked in and took my usual seat on the third row.

He glanced up for a moment as I strolled in, but quickly looked back down at his phone, as if I was just another student and not the girl who'd sucked his cock in the restroom of a dive bar two nights before.

I wasn't terribly disappointed because I wasn't sure what I thought was going to happen when we saw each other this morning.

I didn't expect him to do a happy dance when he saw me.

But I didn't expect to be ignored either.

Honestly, I wasn't sure how to act myself.

Should I be all cold and aloof?

Should I be all cute and flirtatious?

Should we pretend not to know each other so the rest of the room doesn't surmise what happened between us?

Obviously, Logan was going for the "let's pretend like nothing happened" option, so I figured I'd do the same. Once everyone had drifted in and taken their seats, he moved to the chalkboard and started class like he had every other day.

Then, subtly, I noticed the change.

I caught him glancing my way, even when he was addressing the questions of other students.

It was like he knew I was there, watching him, longing for him, and he felt the need to steal a glance because he felt the same way.

He couldn't resist the urge to look at me; to imagine himself fucking me, having me in his arms, his big cock buried deep inside me.

He was feeling the same needs and urges that I was, I was sure of it.

I was sitting in a pool of my own juices, imagining his muscular body beneath the baggy clothes, watching his lips move as he spoke, his nostrils flutter as he breathed.

I squeezed my thighs together and bit my lip.

There was no turning back now.

If I didn't have Logan Clark inside me soon, I might just die.

CHAPTER ELEVEN: Logan

I felt her watching me for the entire class. I did my best to ignore her, but it was no use. I knew she was there. I could feel her eyes on me. I imagined that I could hear breathing. I would have sworn that I noticed the tangy aroma of her juices wafting on the stale air in the room.

I did my best to hold it together for the hour, and was relieved when I finally looked at the clock and saw that it was time for class to end.

I dismissed the class, then sat down behind the desk and waited for the room to clear. I picked up my phone and pretended to fiddle with it. My mouth was dry. I licked my lips. I needed a drink. Maybe I'd run home between classes and grab one. Or two.

"Professor Clark?"

I glanced up to see her standing there, wearing a Golden State Bears t-shirt and a pair of skinny jeans cut low on her hips. The jeans were so tight I could see the outline of her twat. Thank God, she was holding her books in front of her boobs.

I swallowed the lump that had wedged in my throat and folded my hands together on the desk, doing my best to look as academic and uninterested as possible. I lifted my eyebrows at her.

"Yes, Miss Shaw?"

"I have a question about the finals," she said, saying it loud enough so those still drifting from the room could hear. She turned and waited until we were alone, then gave me a smile and set the books on the desk. Her big boobs more than filled out the t-shirt. I could see the outline of her nipples. I subconsciously licked my lips.

"I really just wanted to thank you for the other night," she said, giving me a warm smile, as if she was thanking me for a lovely dinner. "And to let you know that my offer to continue the fun still stands. Anytime. Anywhere."

I rubbed my forehead to drive the thoughts of her lips around my cock out of my mind. I said, "Miss Shaw, look..."

"Call me Courtney," she said. She lowered herself into a chair and crossed her arms on the desk. She rested her boobs on her arms. Her nipples were more apparent now.

"Courtney, look, as flattered as I am to even think that you might be interested in me, we can't take this any farther. There are rules against fraternization between the staff and students."

"So it's okay that you're fucking most of the female professors," she said thoughtfully, "but you can't fuck a female student. Even one who would willingly let you do so."

I blinked at her for a minute. "Who said I was fucking anyone?"

She shrugged. "Come on, Logan. Everybody knows you're fucking the old ladies on staff. It's not a big deal. I certainly won't hold that against you. Actually, that makes it even more exciting for me. I can't wait to see your face when you shove your big cock into a sweet, young, tight, soaked pussy." She batted her eyelashes at me. "You'll never want to fuck old Martha Warner or Sheila Denning again."

I was literally dumbfounded by her words and her knowledge of my extracurricular activities. I sat silent for a moment, waiting for my brain to come up with something to say that would convince her that she was wrong, but no snappy retorts came to mind. I cleared my throat and played innocent badly.

"Um, I'm not sure where you got that information from, but I can assure you that it is patently untrue. I am not involved with anyone on staff here at Golden State." Christ, I sounded like a bad defense lawyer.

She cut her eyes at me. "So you didn't fuck Dean Warner in the Ruby Tuesdays parking lot like everyone is saying? And you and Professor Denning don't fuck at your house every time her husband Coach Denning is coaching away games?"

I stammered a bit. "What? No, I mean, of course, it's not true. And you should tell anyone who is spreading those kinds of malicious rumors that they can get in serious trouble for doing so."

"Relax, Logan, your little secrets are safe with me."

I blinked at her. "Fine. Thank you."

She clicked her tongue and shook her head, then leaned in and lowered her voice. I couldn't help but steal a glance down the front of her shirt. I wanted to run my tongue down her round cleavage.

She said, "This would be so much more fun if we were just honest with one another, don't you think?"

My eyes slowly drifted up to meet hers. I leaned into the desk and lowered my voice. I said, "Fine, I'll be honest with you, Miss Shaw. It's none of your business who I'm fucking because I'm not breaking any rules. I can't afford to lose this job. I'm not willing to risk it, no matter how sweet, young, tight or soaked your pussy might be."

That made her smile, as if she'd just won a hand of cards.

"I understand, Professor Clark," she said with a sigh. She had her bag hanging over her shoulder. She reached inside it and brought out a plastic sandwich baggie. Inside the baggie, was a red thong. She tossed the bag on the desk and nodded at it.

"I was wearing those while I sucked your cock," she said, getting to her feet. "I soaked them through and through while I was sucking you. I thought you might enjoy them as much as I enjoyed you."

With that, she turned and sauntered out of the classroom. I watched the door for a moment, waiting to see if she was going to return. When she didn't, I picked up the baggie and tugged it open. Immediately, the smell of her tangy juices wafted from the baggie. I held the baggie to my nose and closed my eyes to inhale deeply.

The smell of her pussy ignited my senses.

My cock twitched in my pants.

I could taste her on my tongue

I zipped the baggie shut, then put it in my briefcase.

I glanced at the clock. I had an hour before my next class.

Time enough to run home for a drink or two.

Time enough to lie on my bed with Courtney's panties over my nose and mouth and my cock in my hand.

Time enough to do to myself what I was now longing to do to her.

CHAPTER TWELVE: Logan

I had forgotten that I had walked to work. My place was only a few minutes away, but I would have to hurry if I was going to have time to have a drink and jack-off to Courtney's thong.

Wow, what an odd thought to go through your head...

Hmm, what's this entry on my calendar? Why look, at two o'clock I'm slated to have a drink and jack-off to Courtney's thong... I can't miss that again...

Horny idiot.

I had made it just down the street from the accounting building when I saw a familiar blue Honda Accord pass by. The driver hit the brakes and whipped the car into the curb. The passenger window slid down as I approached.

"Hey you," Sheila Denning said, leaning across the seat to call me over. Fuck... not now... I put on a happy face and leaned into the window.

Sheila was in her mid-thirties but looked much younger. She had a full mane of naturally blond hair and big blue eyes. She had a turned-up nose and a set of lips most Hollywood actresses would have killed for.

She was a cheerleader at UCLA and Chuck was on the football team when they got married. She held her looks well, but Chuck was now balding and had a gut like a beach ball. I thought that was one of the reasons Sheila was attracted to me. I was one of the few single, forty-something-year-old guys on staff that didn't look like a walking advertisement for heart failure.

Sheila was wearing a pair of black slacks and a willowy blouse that hid one of the most rocking bodies on campus, regardless of her age. I knew every inch of her body well. I'd gone over it in fine detail with my fingers and my tongue. I was glad that she was happily married to Charlie and just having fun with me. If she had been available, we probably would have hooked up and I knew where that would end.

"Hey yourself," I said, giving her a smile. "Where are you headed?"

"I have a meeting with Dean Warner," she said. "Where are you going?

"Oh, just thought I'd run home for a sandwich." I made a big show of checking my watch. "My next class is in hour, so..."

"Well get in and I'll drop you by your house," she said, giving her head a little jerk.

"Oh, no, I wouldn't want you to go out of your way."

"Nonsense," she said, patting the passenger seat. "It'll take two minutes."

I thought about turning her down, but that would have set off a red flag for her. Sheila was a knockout and a tiger in the sack, but she could also be a jealous bitch and I'd felt her wrath several times in recent months.

Even though she was married, she didn't like me having anything to do with other women. Once, she saw me out with a waitress that I occasionally banged and she went ballistic, leaving threatening messages on my phone and showing up drunk at my house in the middle of the night. She told me that I belonged to her and I'd better not be seeing anyone else.

She'd shit a brick if she knew that I was fucking Dean Warner and a half dozen other women in her faculty group.

I'm not dumb.

I know that the shit will hit the fan someday.

Until then, I'll just keep on lying and fucking her.

And hiding all the sharp objects when she comes to call.

I climbed into the passenger seat and set the briefcase on the floor between my feet. Sheila waited until I buckled up, then pulled away from the curb and headed off campus.

"So, how was your weekend?" she asked.

"Fine. I took the bike up into the mountains," I said. "How was yours?"

"Oh, same old same old," she said with a sigh. She put her hand on my thigh and scratched her nails into my leg. She gave me a sideways glance and smiled. "I missed you."

"You did?"

"Of course," she said, her hand sliding up my thigh toward my crotch. "Didn't you miss me?"

"Of course," I said with a nervous chuckle. Her hand kept inching upward. By the time she pulled to the curb in front of my bungalow, she was rubbing my cock through my pants.

She put the car into gear and turned towards me, leaning her right elbow on the console and putting her left hand on my erection.

"I could come in for a minute," she said, her fingers squeezing and massaging my cock beneath the thin khaki. "I could help you with that."

"I appreciate that," I said, putting my hand on hers to stop the movement. "If you don't stop that, there'll be no need to come inside."

"I can make you come in your pants," she said, trying to wiggle her hand from mine. She gave me a dreamy look and stuck her tongue between her lips.

"I don't think that's a good idea," I said, pushing her hand away and picking up the briefcase to cover my crotch. "I have to get back to class and I don't want to do it with a big wet spot on my pants."

"You're no fun," she said, pouting her lips.

"Now you know that's not true," I said, giving her a sly smile. I reached for the door handle and gave it a tug. "Thanks for the ride."

She grabbed my arm before I could open the door. "Hey, Charlie's away this weekend. I was thinking I'd come over and spend the night on Friday. Maybe you could take me on a bike ride into the mountains on Saturday. Maybe we could take a blanket... have a little picnic... maybe fuck in the woods... like animals..."

"Oh, yeah, that sounds great," I said, pushing open the door with my elbow to make my escape. I slammed the door and leaned back in through the window. "We'll talk before then."

She narrowed her dark eyes at me. "Logan, is anything wrong?"

"Wrong? No, of course not. I'm just in a rush is all."

She stared at me for a moment, like she was trying to read my mind, then gave me a little smile. "Okay, I'm off to meet with Dean Warner. I'll see you later." She dipped her eyes and gave her chin a lift, as if she were looking down at my crotch through the closed door. "Be careful with that thing, Professor. Don't hurt yourself."

I stood with the briefcase covering my erection and waved as she drove away.

It was turning out to be a very interesting day.

The kind of day you look back on as the day before the shit hit the fan.

CHAPTER THIRTEEN: Courtney

"You actually gave him your thong?" Mindy grinned at me from the other side of the lunch table. "Oh my god, Courtney, that's so freakin' awesome. Why don't I ever think to do stuff like that."

"Because all the guys you wanna fuck just say bring it on," I said, biting off the end of a French fry. I picked up a napkin and wiped ketchup from my lips. "Professor Clark is making me work for it, so I have to get creative."

She leaned in with a devilish look in her eyes. "What do you think he'll do with them?"

I picked up the soda cup and brought the straw to my lips. "I dunno. Maybe he'll sleep with them under his pillow. Or jack-off with them stuffed in his mouth."

Mindy chuckled and waved a hand at me. "God, Courtney, you're awful."

"I'm not awful," I said with a playful frown. "I'm just horny."

"If you were just horny, you'd just go get laid," Mindy said matter-of-factly. She glanced around the crowded cafeteria. "There are a dozen guys in here right now who would gladly scratch that itch for you. This thing you have for Logan Clark, it goes much deeper than that. It's not about just getting laid anymore, is it?"

"Oh god, please, not the psycho-babble bullshit again," I said. Mindy was a psych major who hoped to someday have her own psychiatric practice where she could listen to crazy people bitch and moan about their crazy lives all day.

We had been roommates for the last three years and Mindy was constantly trying to psychoanalyze me, like I was her own private lab rat or case study or something. It thrilled her when I told her about my daddy complex, and she was constantly picking apart my various relationships and sexual misadventures, looking for deep, dark undertones that she could dissect and solve for me.

Sometimes it was fun to play along, but other times, when she actually struck a nerve, it was not such fun. I knew I was a mental and sexual basket case. I didn't need my roommate constantly trying to figure out why.

I huffed at her and said, "Honestly, Mindy, I wish you were an art major or something that didn't require you to psychoanalyze me all the time. I'm not your class project, you know."

"Maybe not, but I think there's more here than you just trying to screw an older professor," Mindy said. She put on a thoughtful face as she picked up a French fry and swirled it around the ketchup on her plate. I recognized that face. It was her "I'm staring into your brain" face. I could practically hear the gears turning in her head. She munched on the fry and studied me with her eyes almost closed.

She asked, "Do you ever think about doing more than just having sex with him?"

"What does that even mean?"

"Do you ever think about having a relationship with him that goes beyond just sex? Do you ever think about having a long-term relationship with him?" Mindy picked up her cup and shook the ice, then suctioned out the last noisy sip and cocked her eyebrows at me.

"It's hard to be seriously psychoanalyzed by someone sucking that loudly on a straw," I said, rolling my eyes. "I told you, I just wanna have sex with Logan Clark before I leave for Chicago in a month. That's all there is to it."

"I'm not so sure," she said, slowly nodding, giving me her 'all knowing eye' stare. "I've seen you chase guys before, Court. You've never gone to this much trouble just to get laid."

"Maybe I just like a challenge," I said. "It's not like I'm falling in love with him, Mindy. I just want to have sex him. So please, cut the psychoanalysis before I punch you in the tits."

"Okay, session over," Mindy said, holding up her hands. She glanced at her watch and picked up her lunch tray. "I've got to get to class. Don't do anything crazy without checking with me first. There are stalker laws in this state, you know."

"Very funny, Dr. Ruth," I said. "I'll see you at home."

I watched her make her way through the crowded cafeteria, the short girl with dark curls and a heavy backpack thrown over her shoulder.

Mindy was going to be a fine psychiatrist someday, though I would never admit to her that my fantasies about Logan Clark sometimes did include more than just sex.

I knew it was foolish.

I would be leaving in a month.

I wasn't looking to start a relationship.

I just wanted to get laid.

At least that's what I kept telling myself.

CHAPTER FOURTEEN: Logan

Two days went by and I couldn't get Courtney Shaw off my mind. Even though I hadn't seen or heard from her since she tossed the stained thong on my desk and sauntered out of my classroom, she was constantly there when I closed my eyes to sleep or just tried to turn off my brain at the end of a long day.

I found myself sitting on the couch at midnight with a beer in one hand and the TV remote in the other, blurry eyes directed at the TV but not watching it, my brain in the bedroom with her.

I knew it was pointless to be thinking about her in such a way, but I couldn't help it. She refused to get out of my mind. The image of her smiling up at me with her fingers around my cock and my jizz on her lips played over and over in my head on a loop. Try as I might, I couldn't turn it off.

I had spent my days wondering what it would be like to bury my cock deep inside her and my nights dreaming about doing it. I wanted to feel her warm, soft skin at the tips of my fingers. I wanted to roll her plump nipples between my fingers. I wanted to taste her lips and lick her pussy and feel my cock slowly slipping inside her.

Fuck!!!

Even the alcohol didn't quell my desires or hamper my thoughts. If anything, it made things worse, because the more I drank, the more I thought about her. And the more like shit I felt the next day. Even Tom Brooks noticed the dark circles under my eyes and the puff redness of my cheeks. He had shot me a disapproving look in the hallway this morning, knowing that I was preaching the sins of alcohol to him while baptizing myself in it.

I knew why it was happening.

It was the age-old temptation of man that dated back two thousand years.

I was Adam and Courtney was Eve, holding out the delicious red apple, tempting me to take a bite even though we both knew such things were forbidden by our Lord Golden State University.

Or was she really Lucifer, just using Eve and the apple as tools through which to draw me into temptation, knowing that I would eventually give in and all hell would break loose.

It's the curse of man: we want something we can't have.

And knowing that we can't have it just makes us want it even more.

For men of questionable faith and values, men like me, there comes a point where willpower and consequence are thrown to the wind.

There comes a point where my cock impales itself deep inside her womb and I fill her with my toxic seed.

There comes a point where pleasure is served and consequence begins.

I should have never gone into that restroom.

I should have never let her suck my cock.

I should have never accepted her stained thong, so pungent with her juices and tangy aroma.

I should have never laid naked on my bed with the thong pressed to my face and my hand squeezing the seed from my cock.

But I did.

I did it all.

And now it's all I think about.

Her thong was in my briefcase at that very moment.

I tried, but I could not leave it at home.

I had to have it near me, within easy reach.

I took it into the men's restroom when I got to work that morning and jacked-off into the toilet with the thong between my teeth and the crotch wrapped around my tongue.

Her thong was my new drug of choice.

I could not go very long without a fix.

God help me if her scent ever faded away.

I'm not sure what I would do.

CHAPTER FIFTEEN: Logan

Thursday night… I went straight home after work, resisting the urge to go to Goldie's because I was afraid she might be there. I knew that the only way I could resist her was to keep my distance, to not go where she might be.

I was like an obese person trying to fight the urge to eat: I could only resist scarfing down a bag of Oreos if they weren't in the house. I could only resist Courtney Shaw if she kept away.

I shucked off my work clothes and changed into a pair of running shorts and a t-shirt. I microwaved a burrito and pulled a beer from the fridge. I took my healthy dinner into the living room and slumped on the couch to watch the news. I wasn't really paying attention. It was just noise, a hopeful distraction.

My cellphone was on the coffee table. Midway through the burrito it buzzed with a text message. I wiped my mouth on the back of my hand and picked up the phone.

The text message was from a number I didn't recognize.

The text message read: *Can I cum over?*

I stared at the screen.

The cursor blinked at me.

I read the text again, then leaned forward to brace my elbows on my knees. My hands were shaking.

I typed in: *Who is this?*

She instantly typed back: *You have my thong :o)*

Fuck.

I licked my lips and stared at the screen.

I read the first message again: *Can I cum over?*

I quickly typed: *Sorry busy goodbye.*

I sent the message and tossed the phone on the coffee table, as if it had burned my fingers. I picked up the beer and took a sip. I held my breath and watched the screen, waiting for a reply.

Hoping for a reply.

The phone buzzed. I leaned forward to read the message.

RU 2 busy to open the door?

I blinked at the message, frowning at it with the beer bottle at my lips. What the hell did that mean...

Then the doorbell rang.

Lucifer had arrived.

It was now up to Adam to resist temptation.

CHAPTER SIXTEEN: Courtney

I was already parked at the curb in front of Logan's house when I sent the first text. I typed in and deleted a dozen variations before settling on: *Can I cum over?*

It was cute and suggestive.

Hopefully, it would make him smile.

And maybe a little hard.

I hit send and waited for his reply.

I'd been sitting there for several minutes, watching the house, making sure no one else was following him home. Mindy's comment about California's stalker laws came to mind.

I smiled.

I wasn't a stalker, not in the legal sense.

I wasn't psychotically obsessed with Logan Clark, nor did I mean him any harm. I just wanted to sleep with him. And I knew he wanted to sleep with me. But if he blew me off this time, I'd take the hint and move on. I'd be sad, but I wouldn't bother him again.

My phone buzzed. He texted: *Sorry busy goodbye.*

I smiled. A pathetic attempt at resistance if I'd ever seen one. I gave him a minute to stew, then got out of the car and went to his door.

Standing on his porch, I sent: *RU 2 busy to open the door?*

I imagined him reading the message, perhaps excited and a little frightened that there was just a wooden door between us now.

I held a finger to the doorbell, took a deep breath, and pressed the button. I heard it ding inside the house.

I took a deep breath and stepped back.

What happened next would be up to him.

CHAPTER SEVENTEEN: Logan

I opened the door and there she was, literally the girl of my dreams, standing just a few feet away, so close that I could smell her.

Her red hair cascaded over her shoulders. Her blue eyes sparkled with promise. Her tongue went across her plump lips, making them shine. She was wearing a long black coat and stiletto heels. Somehow, I knew that the only thing under the coat was her luscious body.

"You shouldn't be here," I said, glancing past her to the street. "Someone might see you."

"No one will see me if you let me in," she said playfully. My eyes couldn't resist going up and down her. She had her hands in the pockets of the coat. The coat wasn't buttoned, but it was cinched at the waist by the belt. She brought her hands to the belt and grinned at me. "I'm getting a little warm in this coat. Should I just take it off out here?"

"No, please, don't do that," I said. I could hear the panic in my voice and I knew she could to. I stepped aside and motioned her in. I stepped to the edge of the porch and looked up and down the street. Thank God, I did not see a blue Honda Accord headed my way. Sheila wanted to come over Friday night, but it would not be unlike her to stop by for a quickie between out-of-town games.

"Nice place," she said as I closed and locked the door.

"Courtney, you can't be here," I said, holding up my hands. "We can't do this."

"Yes, Logan, we can. And we must."

The coat came open as she turned to face me. She shrugged it off her bare shoulders and let it fall to the floor.

The breath caught in my throat as my eyes took in her beauty. She was nude, as I expected her to be. Her tits were large and milky white. They hung from her chest, but were round and firm. Her areolas were dark, the size of baseballs. Her nipples were pink and plump, large and suckable. A neatly-trimmed vee of red curls directed my gaze to her clit and pussy lips.

My cock grew hard, pushing out the front of the running shorts.

She glanced down at it and licked her lips.

Without another word, I closed the space between us and pulled her into my arms. The moment our lips touched, I knew we had reached the point of no return.

CHAPTER EIGHTEEN: Courtney

I let the coat fall away and stood naked before him. If he could resist me now, he would be the first to do so. Every lover before him took one look at my big tits and round hips and red bush and fell over themselves to get to me.

Logan looked at me like a deer in headlights. I was a little sad, really, watching him try to resist. I knew there were a thousand thoughts going through his mind. He wanted to fuck me, but he was afraid of anyone finding out and losing his job. I'd never do anything to get him in trouble. This night would be our secret, now and for always.

His desires slowly overtook his fears. His cock grew hard before my eyes, pushing out the thin material of the running shorts. It was at that moment that I knew he would be mine.

He moved quickly, taking me into his arms and pressing his lips to mine. His tongue pushed into my mouth, hot, wet. He tasted like Mexican food and beer... I sighed. I loved Mexican food and beer...

His hands went around my waist and clutched my ass. His fingers dug in hard, kneading my fleshy cheeks, pulling me into his hard cock. I tugged at the t-shirt he was wearing. As he pulled it over his head, I hooked my fingers into the waistband of the shorts and pushed them down his legs.

"Jesus... fuck..." he moaned as his cock sprang free and I took it in my hand. I cupped his balls with my other hand and slowly starting tugging on him, rolling the skin over the rigid shaft.

The head of his cock was thick and round. I swirled it against my tummy. It left a little trail of juices on my skin.

"You want me to fuck you, don't you?" he said, his lips at my ear, his teeth nibbling my earlobe, his hands massaging my tits.

"Yes," I sighed, feeling the hot flow of my cunt. I brought the head of his cock to my clit and swirled it around. "I want you to fuck me, Logan. I want you to fuck me hard."

"You want me to slam my big cock into your sweet pussy," he said.

"Yes..."

"You want me to fuck you till you scream..."

"Yes... please...fuck me..."

He grabbed my ass again and pulled me into him. I got on my tiptoes and spread my thighs. His long cock slid across my pussy, making me jump at the tingle. I lowered myself onto his cock, straddling the long shaft like the bar of a bicycle.

"Fuck, your pussy is so hot," he said, his lips on mine, breathing into my mouth. He put his hands on my waist and rocked his hips, sliding his cock in and out from between my clenched thighs. I shuddered as the head of his cock rolled under my clit, then slid all the way to my asshole. My pussy lips cling to his shaft. My hole gushed hot juices over him, soaking his cock and balls and the insides of my thighs. My scent filled the air.

I reached around and dug my fingernails into his ass. He moaned at the pain.

"God... Logan... you're going to make me cum..."

I moaned the words into his ear as my pussy slid over his shaft. I could feel the orgasm building from deep inside me, like the spark of a fire about to become an inferno. When his shaft slid over my clit again, I couldn't hold back. I grabbed onto his shoulders and lurched my hips into him. I gushed hot juice over him. It dripped from my pussy like an overflowing gutter during a hard rain. He grabbed my ass and pulled me hard into him again as I came.

"Yes, baby," he said. "Cum on my hard cock. Show me how much you love having my cock between your legs."

I clung to him until the orgasm passed. I put my lips to his chest and struggled to catch my breath.

"I want to fuck you now," he said, squeezing my ass so hard I moaned. "I want to jackhammer my cock into your tight, sweet box."

"Then shut up and do it," I said, gazing up at him with a dreamy smile. "Fuck me, Logan. Fuck me now..."

CHAPTER NINETEEN: Logan

I scooped Courtney up into my arms and carried her into my bedroom. She wrapped her arms around my neck and nibbled at my jaw as I pushed open the door with my knee. The place was a mess, of course. The bed was unmade, the sheets hadn't been changed in... ever, clothes were strewn about the floor, crap was everywhere. All I did was sleep and fuck there, so I never saw the need to clean the place up. I'd never really considered the place home anyway.

I set Courtney on the edge of the bed and leaned down to kiss her lips. She stuck out her tongue for me to suck. Her hand immediately went to my stiff cock, still slick from her juices. She slid her hand back and forth quickly, as if she was trying to make me cum. She pressed her lips to the tip of my cock and moaned.

I put my hands on her cheeks and closed my eyes to focus on not cumming so soon. What she was doing with her hands and lips felt amazing, but I wanted to come inside her sweet pussy.

"I want my cock inside of you," I said, putting my hands on her shoulders to push her back. I put my hands on her ankles and lifted her legs up, resting her calves against my chest. She playfully rubbed her feet to my cheeks.

"Squeeze your tits," I said as I reached down to guide my cock head into her hole. She was hot and wet. I swirled the head around, lubing in up, then pushed it to her opening and put my hands on her knees.

"Fuck me..." she said, her hands kneaded her tits, leaving red marks on the milky white globes. She took her long nipples between her fingers and tugged on them, pulling them from her breasts, turning them deep crimson.

I rocked my hips toward her and slid my cock deep into her pussy. She moaned as the breath gusted from her lungs. It was the most amazing feeling, the tightness of her pussy around my girthy cock. It was as if her pussy was gripping my shaft, like tiny fingers, squeezing and milking me.

I held on to her legs and rocked my hips in and out, shoving my cock into her hot, wet box as far as it would go. When I felt the tip of my cock hit her cervix, I pulled out until the head appeared at her lips, then slid in again.

"Fuck..." I moaned. "God... Courtney... your pussy... is so... fucking... tight."

"Tight... young... pussy..." she moaned. "God... I love... your... big cock inside me..."

I could feel the orgasm gathering in my balls with every stroke, building the pressure, like a volcano preparing to blow. I squeezed my eyes shut and concentrated on making her cum first.

I slammed my cock into her. The smell of our sex filled the room. The sound of our flesh slapping together mixed with the gusts of our heavy breathing. I was cumming. There was no holding back. I no longer wanted to.

"Fuck... I'm... fuck... cumming," I moaned. I opened my eyes and gazed down at her. She was biting her bottom lip, smiling at me, panting like a dog with her tongue out.

"Cum with me..." I said. "Cum with me... now..."

"Yessss...." She hissed, bucking her ass against me as her orgasm hit. She opened her mouth and sucked in a few quick breaths, then squeezed her eyes shut and tensed her body.

I thrust into her and she bucked against me. I filled her pussy with my hot milky cum as she gushed waves of hot juices over me, washing my cock and balls and dripping to the bed below.

I pushed my cock as far into her cunt as far as it would go and tightened every muscle in my body until I had no more to give. I blew out a long breath, my body collapsing like a deflating balloon. I opened my eyes to find her smiling up at me. She held out her arms, beckoning me to lie down with her.

And I did, knowing it was just the start of what might become the greatest night of my life.

CHAPTER TWENTY: Courtney

"So, you wanted to be a writer, but instead you became an accounting professor." I picked up the steaming hot cup of coffee Logan had made for me and gave him a playful frown. "Exactly how did that happen?"

Logan was sitting on the other side of his little kitchen table with his shirt off. He was nibbling at a strawberry Pop-Tart as he waited for his coffee to cool. His muscled shoulders and chest rippled when he shrugged.

"I quickly learned that most writers starve," he said with a smile. "I liked to eat, so I became an academic. My plan was to write the great American novel in my spare time."

"Are you still working on the novel?" I asked, letting my eyes go around his handsome face. His eyes were a little red. His hair was mussed like a little kid who had just crawled out of bed. The thick stubble shadowed his cheeks and chin.

"No, I don't remember the last time I wrote anything other than the occasional bad check," he said, sadly. He picked up his cup and blew a cooling breath over the steaming coffee. He arched his eyebrows at me. "What about you? What's your plan after graduation?"

I was wearing one of his t-shirts and a pair of his boxers to keep myself from leaking on the chair. My pussy was raw and wet from our night of unbridled fun. It needed a good airing out. I brought up my legs and wrapped my arms around them, then set my chin on my knees.

"Well, my plan is to move to Chicago and work with my step-dad at his accounting firm. I'll work on my MBA at night and eventually, hopefully, make partner before I'm thirty." I frowned at my own words. "Wow, I had no idea how incredibly boring that sounded until I said the words out loud."

He gave me a cautious smile. "Don't you want to be an accountant?"

I blinked at him without answering. If he had asked me that question yesterday I would have immediately said yes, I want to be an accountant. This morning, sitting across from him after a long night of making love, I wasn't sure what I wanted anymore. What the fuck...

I gave him a shrug. "Sure, I mean, math is easy for me, so..."

"Is that why you chose accounting? Because math was easy?" He took a noisy slurp of coffee and arched his eyebrows. "That's surprising."

"Why is that?"

"Because you impress me as a girl that never does anything because it's easy."

My eyes drifted away from his. I stared into the coffee cup on the table between my hands. "I'm not really sure why I chose accounting," I said slowly. "I mean, I'm good at math and my step-dad is an accountant, but is that what I want to do with my life..." I glanced up at him. "Now, I don't know."

He gave me a reassuring smile. "Well, you're young. You have your whole life ahead of you."

"What about you?" I asked, turning the tables on him. "Is this how you plan to spend the rest of your life? Teaching accounting, screwing female professors, getting drunk with Professor Brooks."

His forehead furrowed for a moment and I thought I might have pissed him off. Then his lips curled into a smile and he shook his head. "Gee, you make it sound awful."

I studied his face. "Is it? Awful?"

He took a deep breath and lifted his chin, letting his eyes go around the wall above my head. He was thinking about the question. Maybe he was coming to the same realization that I had; that a life lived by routine can be boring as fuck.

Before he could answer, we heard the front door open. We glanced at each other for a moment, then he got to his feet to see who was coming in.

"Well, well, well, what is going on here?" Professor Denning said, standing in the kitchen door with her arms crossed over her chest. She gave me a hateful glance, then glared at Logan with an intense look of anger on her face. She lowered her eyes to Logan's cock and clicked her tongue. "Fucking your students now, Logan?"

Logan looked down, realizing at that moment that he was standing before her naked with his long cock dangling between his legs.

"How did you get in?" he asked.

"I borrowed your extra key," she said, holding up the key between two fingers. "I had a copy made, in case of emergencies."

"You had no right to do that," Logan said, making no move to cover himself. He held out his hand. "Give me the key."

"We'll discuss that," she said, glancing at me again. "After your little slutty friend leaves."

"Don't call her that," Logan said. His face was turning red. His voice had a twinge of anger that I'd never heard before. His open hand had closed into a fist.

"I'd better go," I said, easing up from the table and sliding past her to get to the bedroom, leaving Logan alone to face her wrath.

I could hear her yelling as I gathered up my clothes and slipped quietly out the front door.

I felt awful, leaving him that way, but I knew this was a battle he would have to face alone because my presence would only make things worse.

I hurried to my car and drove away.

I had to find Mindy as quickly as possible.

I desperately needed a session with my shrink.

CHAPTER TWENTY-ONE: Logan

I felt like a little bit like a kid who'd been sent to the principal's office, sitting with my knees pressed together and my hands folded in my lap, waiting for Dean Martha Warner to determine my fate.

It was incredibly awkward, and more than a little ironic, that the fate of my academic career at Golden State rested in the hands of a woman who had sucked my cock in a Ruby Tuesday's restroom, fucked me in the back of her Volvo in the parking, and commanded me to come home with her so I could, "bang the shit out of her pussy with my monster cock".

But apparently, that was the case, thanks to Sheila Denning and her decision to report my fraternization with a student to the dean.

I warned Sheila that everyone's dirty laundry would come out if she reported me, but that didn't seem to be of much concern to her. She was more determined to have me kicked out of Golden State for cheating on her (what???) than to protect her own rocky marriage.

"Just wait until Chuckie hears what you did to me," she growled, standing in my kitchen with her hands twisted into claws. "He's gonna kick your fucking ass, Logan. He's gonna beat the living shit out of you and I'm gonna be cheering him on!"

Jesus, what a fuck nut. Pity she was so good in bed.

She made good on her threat to report me to the dean that day, though she didn't know she was turning me into a woman I had been fucking for months.

So far, her fat fuck of a husband hadn't shown up at my door or in my classroom, so obviously, he didn't care nearly as much about me fucking his wife as she thought he would.

I was pretty sure Chuck had his own side thing going. Most of the coaches did. He would have probably thanked me for keeping Sheila out of his hair. If he had hair.

I was glad to hear that Courtney wasn't too shaken up by Sheila barging in on us, because I wanted to see Courtney again. Our night together had been amazing, and I didn't want it to be our last.

There were just two weeks left in the semester. After that, Courtney would graduate and we would be able to see each other without restrictions, if that's what she wanted.

I couldn't help but wonder if now that she had fucked me, would she forget me and move on. It was certainly a possibility. One of the reasons I don't chase after younger girls is that most of them love to play schoolgirl games. Older women, women my age, are tired of playing games. They've been there, done that, got the divorce. Older women were also more appreciative and willing to please, whereas girl's Courtney's age could be childish, pouty, and demanding.

I didn't get that impression of Courtney from our one night together, but I knew that first impressions don't mean shit when it comes to women.

Martha laced her fingers together on the desk and blew out a heavy sigh. She made a scolding face. "Really, Logan. Did you have to sleep with Sheila Denning, too? Of all people?"

I frowned at her. "Shouldn't you be asking about the student I slept with?"

She rolled her eyes and waved a hand at me. "For Christ sake, Logan, if I had to fire every professor that was banging a student, this college would be a ghost town." She leaned over the desk and lowered her husky voice. "I would have been fired years ago."

I really liked Martha. She made me smile. I said, "So, why am I here then if it's no big deal?"

Her big breasts bounced as she exhaled. "Because Sheila has gone over my head to press the point with the ethics committee," she said. "And I have no control over them."

I leaned forward and put my elbows on her desk. I held out my fingers like I was about to start counting. "So even though I was fucking Sheila Denning – and you..."

She held up her fingers, counting for me. "And Beverly Moss and Elaine Strickland and Paula Pounders and Eva Mendez and Joan Osborne... and..." She frowned at me. "Am I forgetting anyone?"

I felt a smile come to my lips. "How did you know?"

"Oh, for fuck's sake, Logan, this is a big school in a very small town," she said with a dismissive wave. "We all knew that you were having sex with us, well, all of us besides Sheila, who we knew was a crazy, jealous bitch so we never said anything. We all used to sit in the faculty lounge comparing notes about you."

I fell back in the chair, amusingly stunned. "Well, son of a bitch... I've never felt so... used."

She chuckled and slapped her hands on the desk. "Ah. Logan, you're as funny as you are sexy. Anyway, if it was up to me I'd tell you to go back to work and keep your cock out of Courtney Shaw until she graduates. Then, you can fuck to your heart's content."

"But it's not up to you."

She blew out a long sigh. "Sadly, no. It's up to the ethics committee, which is comprised of two female professors that you probably haven't had sex with because they're ancient, and two male professors, all tenured with the ability to terminate your employment at will. Or to let you remain on staff without tenure."

"Well, crap," I said, rubbing my eyes. "Who are the men?"

She stuck a pair of reading glasses on her nose and stared at her computer screen. "For this term... it's Professors Hughes and Brooks."

I clenched my jaw to keep the smile at bay. "Tom Brooks?"

"Yes," she said, taking off the glasses. "Do you know him?"

"Vaguely," I said. "We've chatted once or twice, at faculty functions."

"Well, then that's it. The ethics committee will meet later today and make their recommendation to me, which I am bound to carry out." She cocked her head and gave me a warm smile. "I hope things go your way, Logan. This campus would not be the same without you."

CHAPTER TWENTY-TWO: Courtney

Shit.

I was just finishing a salad in the cafeteria when my cellphone buzzed and my mom's happy image appeared on the screen. She was calling to talk about graduation and my move home to Chicago.

She and my stepdad, Earl, were planning on flying out to see me cross the stage and pack up my stuff to ship back to Chicago. Only now, I wasn't so sure I wanted to move back home. Or go to work as an accountant. As of this moment, with Logan's job up in the air and no idea what our future might hold – if anything—I didn't know what I wanted to do.

I picked up the phone, took a minute to take a deep breath and muster a fake smile, then swiped to answer the video call.

"Hi mom," I said, smiling into the camera. "How are you?"

"I'm fine, dear. How's it going there?"

"Fine, just busy studying for finals next week."

"You'll do great, dear," she said, giving me her "you can do anything you want" smile. "Are you all packed?"

"No, mom, I still have a couple of weeks to go."

"Oh, well, I just thought that you would be so excited to move back to Chicago and start your new job that you'd already be packing."

"No, not yet." I forgot that she could see me. When I rubbed my eyes and looked away, her voice took on an air of concern.

"What's wrong, sweetie. Haven't you been sleeping well?"

"I'm fine, mom," I said with a tired sigh. I didn't tell her that I'd be a lot better if I could sleep in Logan's arms every night, but for now, we had to be cool. I took a deep breath and gave her a reassuring smile. "I'm just tired. Lots going on. Finals are going to be a fucking bitch."

"Courtney, watch your language," she said, talking to me like I was a little girl. "I hope you remember to not talk like that when you start work with Earl."

"I'll be sure not to saying fucking bitch in front of clients, mom," I said, rolling my eyes.

She narrowed her eyes at me, like she could read my mind across the thousands of miles. "Courtney, is there something wrong? You're not having second thoughts about coming home to work for Earl are you? Oh my god, you're not thinking of staying there in California, are you?"

I didn't answer quickly enough for her, so she pounced.

"Oh, Courtney, please don't tell me you're thinking about backing out. Not after everything Earl has done for you."

"Mom, I'm not backing out," I said. "I'm just thinking about my future. I'm not sure I want to spend the next forty years crunching numbers for a living."

"But you're so good at math, dear," she said. "Your degree will be in accounting. What else would you do?"

"I don't know, mom," I said. "Like I said, I'm not backing out. I'm just thinking about the future."

"Are you, Courtney?" I could see her face getting red on the little video screen. "Are you really thinking or are you doing what you always do?"

"What do I always do, mother?"

"You're like a distracted child sometimes," she said, talking with her hands so the video screen became a jumpy blur. "You set your sights on one thing, then something else gets your attention and you chase that for a while, then something else..." She brought the phone back to her face. "Oh no, let me guess, this is about a boy, isn't it?"

"No, mom, it's not about a boy," I said, making a pissy face at her. I bit my tongue before I could say, "It's about a man!"

She huffed into the phone. "Oh my lord, not again."

I clenched my teeth and glanced around the cafeteria to make sure no one was close enough to hear us. I growled at her. "What does that mean?"

She shook her head and sighed. She was holding the phone so close to her face that all I could see were her eyes. They were welling with tears.

She said, "Courtney, sometimes you think with your vagina rather than your brain. And it never ends well."

I couldn't help but smile. "Mom! Seriously?"

She was still shaking her head. She was sniffing back tears. "I'm sorry for whatever I did when you were young to make you think that your happiness relies on a man, Courtney. I know all about the things you did in high school, things you've probably done in college. The truth is, I did them, too, at your age. I was selfish and promiscuous and always making bad decisions based on the boy of the moment. If Earl hadn't come along to save us both, I honestly don't know what would have happened to us."

"I'm not doing that," I said defensively. The lie that sprung from my lips left a very bad taste in my mouth.

She wiped her eyes. "You're smart, you're beautiful, and you have your whole life ahead of it. Don't do what I did, Courtney. Don't let some infatuation with a boy cause you to throw away everything you've worked so hard to achieve. Trust me, it's just not worth it."

She hung up without saying another word, leaving me staring through tears at the blank screen as my mind wondered if she was right.

CHAPTER TWENTY-THREE: Logan

I was in my classroom, getting ready to administer the last final of the year, when Tom Brooks walked in. He looked great compared to the last time I'd seen him. His eyes were clear and bright with no dark bags hanging from beneath them. He was wearing a new suit and tie. His hair was freshly cut and his skin had a sun-kissed glow. I did a double-take when he came into the room.

"Tom, you look great," I said, getting up to shake his hand.

"Thanks," he said with a proud smile. "I took your advice. Got out of town for the weekend, got some sun. And I've quit drinking and carousing; something you should seriously think about doing."

I thought about feigning ignorance, but just let the comment go. We both knew the truth about me. It was useless to deny it. I held out a hand to motion him to a chair while I sat back down behind the desk.

"So, I suppose you're here to deliver my sentence," I said with a long sigh. "Give it to me straight. I can take it."

He reached inside his jacket and pulled out a folded sheet of paper. "I am here to deliver the ruling of the ethics committee," he said formally. He unfolded the paper and slid it across the desk to me. At the top of the page were the words: ETHICS COMMITTEE RULING.

He said, "The good news is, you are not being fired. Your job, for the moment at least, is safe. There will be no suspension since we are at the end of term. The committee does recommend that you take the summer break to reflect on your actions, and take steps to ensure that such an egregious violation of the rules never happens again."

"In other words, keep it in my pants." I grinned at him, but his face remained somber.

"The bad news is, you will not receive tenure this year."

I picked up the paper and frowned at it. "Fuck. No tenure means I can be terminated or laid off at any time."

"It does," he said, sighing again, as if he had just returned from a long battle. "But you've worked three years without tenure, so unless you fuck up again, you should be fine. The topic of tenure will be revisited on your five-year anniversary... if you're around that long."

I grimaced at his words, like a convict listening to a judge tell him how long he must be in prison before becoming eligible for parole.

I had wanted tenure not because it meant lifetime employment. I had wanted tenure because it offered protection for lazy fuckup academics like me. It was virtually impossible to be fired when you had tenure, no matter your crimes. Tenure was like a license to quit giving a fuck. Most of the tenured professors just went through the motions. Hell, most of them didn't even show up to teach their own classes. They had teaching assistants do it for them. They spent their time writing and publishing papers, and making side money as high-paid consultants for tech companies in the valley.

Tenure was like Willy Wonka's Golden Ticket. Get one and you not only get a free tour of the factory, but you might one day own the whole shebang; or at least be allowed to act like you do. I had desperately wanted tenure, but not as much as I had wanted Courtney Shaw.

"Oh well," I said, working up a smile. "All I have to do is keep my nose clean for two more years."

"It's not your nose that worries me," he said seriously. "My advice to you, my friend, is to keep you dick out of your students. And out of the faculty ladies, especially crazy bitches like Sheila Denning."

I grinned at him. "Point well taken, my friend. I appreciate you going to bat for me."

"Least I could do," he said. "I was headed down a pretty dark road. If you hadn't interceded, well, I might be the one getting fired for some dastardly deed."

"You're going to be fine," I said. I opened my briefcase and slid the paper inside. My nostrils flared as the scent of Courtney's thong wafted from the case. I quickly closed and latched lid, as if I were afraid the scent might escape like a playful spirit.

"What about you?" he asked with a frown.

I blinked at him. "What about me?"

"When are you going get yourself straight, Logan?"

I leaned back and spread my hands. "I have no idea what you're talking about, Tom."

"Come on, Logan, this is me," he said, leaning his elbows on the desk. "I know you're a drunk. The entire time you were preaching the evils of alcohol to me I could smell the booze on your breath. And the lecture you gave me about willpower was total horseshit. I have to believe the booze led you to sleep with a student, because the Logan Clark that I know would have never crossed that line. You're becoming a pathetic shell of the man you used to be. You're a good man. I hate to see you do that to yourself."

I gave him a sideways frown. "What does that mean?"

He got to his feet and dusted off his hands, as if talking to me had left them dirty. He said, "That means that you need to dry out and grow up, Logan. Isn't that what you told me? Though your advice was very much 'do as I say and not as I do.'"

I pushed myself out of the chair and planted my knuckles on the desk. I gave him a hard look. "Have I somehow offended you, Tom?"

"Yes, Logan, you have offended me greatly because for the last three years I've watched a brilliant man piss his life away for booze and pussy," he said, bracing his knuckles on the desk to stand nose-to-nose with me. "You might as well just go home and blow your brains out right now. Just get it over with. Kill yourself quickly and save everyone the pain of watching you do it slowly."

I wanted to punch him in the face.

I wanted to get so fucking angry that I jerked him over the desk and stomped his brains into the floor.

I wanted to tell him that he was wrong and to go to hell.

I wanted to do all those things, but I couldn't.

Because he was right.

I had spent the last three years burrowing myself into a deep, dark hole of booze and women, with no regard for anyone's feelings, not even my own. Then she came along...

"What are you hiding from, Logan?" he asked, his tone softening.

It was a great question, one I avoided asking myself.

When I didn't offer an answer, he said, "Tell me. Why are you here, teaching accounting to college kids that don't give a shit, living in poverty, drinking yourself stupid every night, having sex with women who are happy to fuck you, but wouldn't be seen in public with you? The Logan Clark I met three years ago had so much potential, and now... I have never seen a more miserable son of a bitch in my life."

"Then maybe you should look in the mirror," I said quietly. I threw my hands in the air and yelled at him. "Get on back to Goldie's, Tom. Climb on your stool and get shitfaced while you annoy the shit out of everyone with the story of how you walked in on your wife fucking a three-hundred-pound, black football player!"

He blinked at me for a moment. I thought he was going to hit me. I would have let him do it. I clenched my jaw and dropped my hands to my sides. Hit me, motherfucker. Do it. I deserve it.

He pushed himself away from the desk and took a deep breath. He said, "It's time you took your own advice, Logan. Dry out. Grow up. Find a nice woman your own age and settle down."

He walked to the door, but paused before going through it.

"If you fuck up again, there won't be anything I can do to save you. If you truly like working here, keep your cock in your pants and your mind on the work. Otherwise, save us both the headache and just move on."

CHAPTER TWENTY-FOUR: Logan

The moment Tom left, I called Courtney to give her the good news. No tenure, but my job was safe, she would graduate in a few weeks, and we could be together.

Her phone went straight to voicemail.

"Hey, it's me," I said. "I have good news. Guess I'll just tell you about it when you come to class. I... I'll see you soon."

* * *

Courtney didn't show up for class, even though I was administering the final exam. She was the top student in the class and could graduate without taking the exam, but I never imagined that she would skip it. The one thing she took seriously was her studies.

I asked the other students if they'd seen her.

They all gave me a knowing smirk and said no.

I handed out the final exam and sat at my desk with my phone between my hands.

I sent her a test: *hey r u ok?*

The cursor blinked, but she never texted back.

CHAPTER TWENTY-FIVE: Courtney

I spent the rest of the day locked in my room, thinking about my future. And about Logan Clark, the older professor who was supposed to just be my last conquest before leaving school to start my new life in Chicago.

The plan was to seduce him, fuck him, and move on.

It was the same plan I'd executed flawlessly countless times over the years, starting with my English teacher in tenth grade.

The plan was never to have feelings for him.

The plan was never to imagine myself being with him longer than a few hours.

The plan had gone to shit.

I had feelings for him.

Feelings I'd never felt before.

Feelings that scared the shit out of me.

My mother's words echoed in my head. *You're smart, you're beautiful, and you have your whole life ahead of it. Don't do what I did, Courtney. Don't let some infatuation with a boy cause you to throw away everything you've worked so hard to achieve. Trust me, it's just not worth it.*

Mindy knocked on my door. I told her I was okay. She knew it was a lie, but she left me alone. I guess a good psychiatrist knows that sometimes the patient must work things out for themselves.

My phone buzzed. It was Logan calling. I sent the call to voicemail. A few minutes later, I listened to the message: *Hey, it's me... I have good news. Guess I'll just tell you about it when you come to class. I... I'll see you soon.*

I listened to the message with tears in my eyes.

I listened to it again.

And again.

He sounded so happy.

So relieved.

I deleted the voicemail.

An hour later, my phone buzzed again, this time he had sent a text: *hey r u ok?*

My fingers hovered over the tiny keyboard for a moment.

I read the text again.

I didn't know how to answer the question because I didn't know if I was okay.

My phone buzzed again.

It was my mother calling.

"Fuck," I said, wiping my eyes. I took a deep breath and forced myself to answer the call.

"Hi, mom... yes... I know... you're right... I was just getting cold feet... I know... I love you, too... hey, I was thinking about skipping graduation and coming home now... yes... it's just a formality... they can mail the diploma to me... no, it's not a big deal... okay... I'll book a ticket now and see you soon... okay... I'll email you my itinerary... okay... I love you, too."

I hung up the phone and blew out a long breath.

Mom was right.

I couldn't let my infatuation with Logan Clark change the course of my life.

We used each other, we had a good time, and now it was time to move on.

I opened my laptop and booked a flight home.

CHAPTER TWENTY-SIX: Courtney

One month later... Chicago...

"Hey, Court, how is the Burnham Financial audit coming?" Earl asked, standing in the doorway of my tiny office on the twentieth floor of the Rand Building in Chicago. The office was small, but I had a spectacular view of the river. I looked up at him and smiled.

"It's coming along fine," I said. I spread out my hands at the stacks of files on my desk. "I should have the final report for you by Monday afternoon."

Earl rubbed his hands together and gave me a fatherly grin. "Excellent, I'll let them know." He started to leave, but turned back with a finger sticking in the air. "Oh, your mom is cooking spaghetti Friday night. Can we expect to see you there?"

"Of course," I said, mustering a smile for his benefit. "You're just a short train ride away."

"Fantastic," he said, checking his watch. "It's almost six. You should get out of here."

"I will. I'm wrapping things up now."

He blew me a kiss and disappeared down the hallway.

I thought about working for another hour or two. It wasn't like I had anything better to do. I could go to my apartment and unpack boxes, I supposed. Or grab a bite at one of the restaurants between here and there. No, scratch that. I hated to eat alone. I always felt like such a loser.

I stared at the stack of files for a moment, but decided I'd had enough. I shut down my computer, switched off the light, and headed for home.

CHAPTER TWENTY-SEVEN: Courtney

I changed into a pair of baggy sweat pants and a Golden State t-shirt, then padded barefoot into the kitchen of my new apartment to forage dinner from the fridge.

I opened the fridge to find that it contained half a leftover pepperoni pizza and three bottles of beer. My mother would have been horrified by my lack of planning and domestic skills. Her fridge was always overflowing with things to eat. I barely had enough food to keep a bird alive.

I microwaved the pizza and popped the cap off a beer, then sat down with a legal pad and pen to work up a grocery list as I ate. I was halfway through the first slice of pizza when the doorbell rang.

I rubbed my greasy hands on the legs of my sweats as I went to the door. I leaned in to look through the peephole. My breath caught in my throat. On the other side of the door stood Logan Clark.

CHAPTER TWENTY-EIGHT: Logan

When Courtney opened the door, she looked like she was seeing a ghost. I gave her my best "SURPRISE!" smile and said, "Hi, Courtney.

"Logan, what are you doing here?" she asked.

"I was just in the neighborhood, so I thought I'd drop by," I said. "It took me three planes, an airport shuttle, and a taxi to get to the neighborhood, but here I am."

She leaned against the door and blinked at me. I couldn't tell if she was happy to see me or not. "I don't understand. Why are you here?"

"I just needed to know what happened," I said, letting my shoulders go up and down. "I'm not here expecting anything. I just need to know what I did to drive you away."

* * *

"You didn't do anything to drive me away," Courtney said after letting me in and leading me to the sofa. I sat on one end, she sat on the other.

"Then what happened?" I asked. "Why did you leave without saying goodbye?"

Her beautiful eyes closed and she took a quick breath. She opened her eyes and spoke quietly. "I had my whole life planned out, Logan. I couldn't let what happened between us change that. I thought it would be easier for both of us if I just left. I also didn't want to get you into any more trouble or give you a reason to make a decision based on what happened between us."

"Why did you think I would do that?" I asked. "I mean, we had one amazing night together, and seemed to enjoy each other's company, but I had no expectations. We were just getting to know each other. It never occurred to me that you would change your plans for me."

She narrowed her eyes at me. "You weren't having... feelings for me? I mean, I got the impression from your voicemail... shit... did I misread things that badly?"

I hadn't come this far to lie to her. I said, "I won't deny that I was incredibly attracted to you, or that I wanted to spend more time with you. I mean... I might have been feeling something... I mean... I wasn't in love with you then..."

Her mouth slowly opened. "Then?"

I took a deep breath and let it out slowly. It didn't ease the tension that I felt in every muscle of my body. I hadn't had a drop of alcohol in a month. Things seemed so much easier when I was stoned.

I said, "I'm not saying that I'm in love with you. And I'm not saying that I'm not."

Her eyes softened as they went around my face. "Then what are you saying?"

"I'm saying that I can stay in Chicago for a month before I have to be back at work," I said, giving her a hopeful look. "Maybe we can spend some time together, get to really know one another. Now that we aren't governed by some silly rule about fraternizing with a student."

"So you want to fraternize with me as an adult," she said, her lips curling into a smile.

"Yes," I said, holding out a hand and praying she'd take it. "I'd like that very much."

She slipped her hand into mine and smiled.

"Very well, Professor Logan. Fraternize away."

CHAPTER TWENTY-NINE: Courtney

Logan took my hand and pulled me across the couch. I pressed my lips to his as we tore at each other's clothing; kicking off shoes, tugging shirts over heads, pushing pants and underwear down legs.

When we were naked, he leaned back on the couch with his big cock sticking straight up like the mast of a great ship. I sat next to him for a moment, our tongues dueling, his fingers dipping into my flowing pussy, my fingers wrapping around his cock.

I pumped him for a minute, then he put his hands on my shoulders and pulled me over on top of him. I straddled his legs and put my hands on his shoulders.

He held his cock steady as I slowly lowered my pussy onto him. The moment the head of his cock hit my opening, I nearly came. My juices washed over him like a hard rain, soaking his cock and balls, lubricating his way inside me.

Logan put his hands on my tits and I rolled my hips back and forth, milking his cock back and forth, rolling my tender clit over the top of the shaft. Sparks of lightning shot through me. I dug my fingers into his shoulders as he tweaked my nipples and buried his mouth into my neck.

"God... I missed you..." I moaned. My body tingled as my pussy tightened around him. The orgasm was coming quickly. I could feel him in cunt, my chest, my throat, my heart, my mind.

"I'm cumming..." he moaned, moving his hands to my hips to rock me faster over his cock. The muscles in his shoulders rippled as he threw back his head and howled. "God... Court... cum..."

I closed my eyes and rode him like a bucking bronco, taking his cock in as far as it would go before letting it slide out. My clit vibrated over the shaft. I curled my toes and dug my teeth into his shoulder.

"Logan... oh... god... Logan..."

Our bodies tensed together for a minute, then relaxed.

I leaned forward with his cock still inside me and wrapped my arms around his neck.

"I'm so glad you showed up," I said, smiling, nibbling at his ear. A sudden thought made me frown. I pulled back to look him in the eye. "How did you find me?"

He smiled. "Your friend Mindy came to my house," he said. "She seemed worried about you, moving to the big city all alone."

"Really?" I grinned. I still talked to Mindy almost every day. She was now my remote shrink. "And she said you should come check on me?"

He shrugged with his eyes. "She just said if I was ever in Chicago I should look you up. She gave me your address. She thought you might be glad to see me."

"Well, she was right," I said, pressing my forehead to his. "That Mindy, she always knows how to make me feel better."

"And do you feel better?" he asked, gazing into my eyes.

"Yes, Logan, I do. Now shut up and kiss me again."

EPILOGUE: Logan

I never returned to California. After a month, I called Martha Warner and turned in my resignation. Then I called Tom Brooks and told him he could have my motorcycle if he would clean out the bungalow and just donate everything to charity.

I had no reason to return.

Everything I cared about was right here, right now.

Courtney worked during the day while I sat at her apartment and worked on my new book.

Yes, that's right, I was writing again, after nearly twenty years.

I had saved enough money to live for a couple of years, so Courtney convinced me to take time off to write a book.

It was a love story about an older man who was stumbling blindly through life, and the younger woman who took him by the hand and heart and showed him the way to happiness.

It was an easy book to write because it was the story that I was living every day.

Now, if I could just get Courtney's mother to like me, all would be right with the world.

THE END

Don't miss out!

Visit the website below and you can sign up to receive emails whenever Amy Brent publishes a new book. There's no charge and no obligation.

https://books2read.com/r/B-A-GACH-HIPMB

BOOKS 2 READ

Connecting independent readers to independent writers.

Did you love *Filthy Professor*? Then you should read *Filthy Seal*[1] by Amy Brent!

[2]

I'm a former Navy SEAL and mercenary for hire. I'm one disciplined, hard-nosed, tough as nails, son of a bitch. And I've fought bad guys all over the word... Iraq... Afghanistan... Pakistan... Africa... I'm not afraid of any man or anything. Nothing rattles me. Nothing. Then I learn that my wife is dead back in the states and my regimented world is turned upside down. She's not only dead, but she's dead with another guy's baby in her womb. And deep inside, I know it could be my fault.

Ben Ryder... Fine, I'll admit it. I was never the best husband or father. In ten years of marriage I was gone a lot, leaving Bethany to hold down the fort and raise our son, Cody, all alone. But that's the life of a SEAL's wife, the life she signed up for. When I shipped out two

1. https://books2read.com/u/3yzYNJ

2. https://books2read.com/u/3yzYNJ

months ago she told me she wanted a divorce. Now I learn that she died while carrying another guy's baby. It was not quite the homecoming I'd hoped for, especially when I learn that her death might not have been an accident as everyone first thought.

Then I meet her, Lolita, the hot nineteen-year-old sex kitten next door. I spy on her when she's alone in her backyard pool, floating naked on a raft with her fingers busy between her legs. She knows I'm watching her. Touching myself. My hand in rhythm with hers. I know she can feel my eyes burning into her body like the laser sight on my assault rifle.

Soon, she's in my bed and in my life, a wonderful distraction at a horrible time. I should be awash in guilt and sadness, but it's hard to be sad when Lolita wraps her long, lovely legs around my waist and begs me to take her over the moon. In her arms, I feel like the luckiest man alive, at least until reality sets back in and the truth about my wife's death is slowly revealed...

Lolita Carter... My mother named me after that girl in the movie, Lolita. You know the one, it's about this teenage girl who seduces a much older man and slowly drives him insane. I'm not out to drive anyone crazy—at least not like that— but I can't help the things I feel and do when I know the hot Navy SEAL next door is watching me. I know his wife just died, but looking at his muscled chest and shoulders and handsome face just makes me melt in my bikini bottoms. I kept help that I'm just nineteen-years-old in a body like this, with the sex drive of a nymphomaniac and a craving for older men. But I get the feeling he feels the same way I do. There is something about the way he looks at me, the way he licks his lips when his eyes drift slowly over my body. He's a dirty boy, all right, a Filthy SEAL. And I want to be his dirty girl.

Also by Amy Brent

Filthy

Filthy Boss

Filthy Doctor

Filthy Professor

Filthy Seal

Filthy Cowboy

Filthy Daddy

Filthy Coach

Forbidded

The Doctor's Fake Marriage

Forbidden

Fake Fiance

One More Chance

Crave Me

My Best Friend's Dad

The Doctor's Fake Marriage

Dad's Best Friend

Forbidden Fantasies

Daddy's Business Partner

Daddy's Friend

Daddy O

Climbing His Corporate Ladder

Taken By Daddy's Boss

Filthy Liar

Standalone

Teachers' Pet

Filthy Box Set

Knocked Up By My Brother's Best Friend

My Best Friend's Brother

My Best Friend's Ex

Say You're Mine

Club Desire Box Set

My Boyfriend's Dad

Fighting For Her

Forbidden Love Box Set

Love Undercover

Friends With Benefits

A Royal Menage

Baby Fever

Vegas Baby

Brother's Best Friend for Christmas

Christmas With My Best Friend's Dad

My Son's Sitter

Single Dad's Christmas Present

Surrendering To 3 Alphas

Because I Love You
Catching Up With Daddy
Claiming Cinderella
Double Trouble
First Love
First Time
Knocked Up By My Brother's Best Friend
My Best Friend's Boyfriend
Pretend Daddy
Redemption
Roomies With Benefits
Royally Yours
Rub Me The Right Way
Show Stopper
That One Night
The Baby Contract
Truth Or Dare
Santa's Naughty List
Quickie on Christmas
Con Man

Printed by Libri Plureos GmbH in Hamburg,
Germany